A Cof. ⌐⌐⌐ᵧ ⌐ᵧᵧˢᵗᵉ⌐ᵧ –
Maddie Goodwell 3

By

Jinty James

CHAPTER 1

"Oh, wow," Maddie Goodwell murmured as she stepped into the hotel ballroom. Numerous stations, each equipped with an espresso machine, greeted her gaze.

The cream-colored walls and ceiling provided a neutral backdrop, and rows of black folding chairs were set out for the public to watch the competition.

"Exactly." Suzanne Taylor, her best friend since middle school, sounded subdued for a second, before her blue eyes lit up. "This is so exciting! And your badge says you're number eight." She pointed to the white badge the registration clerk had given to Maddie a few minutes earlier, which she'd pinned to her lilac shirt.

Maddie nodded, her stomach squirming with anxiety. Yes, it was exciting, but it was also … scary.

Today was the day the Seattle barista championships were being held. The winner of today's event would go on to

1

compete in the nationals. Just the thought of that possibility made Maddie's nerves shred even more.

"It's certainly different to last month's competition in Estherville," Maddie said in a low voice.

Suzanne nodded. "But you won then, and I don't see why you can't win today, either. Your coffee skills are awesome, Maddie. And I'll be in the crowd, cheering you on."

Maddie managed a smile, glad of her friend's encouragement.

Last month in Estherville, the small town one hundred miles from Seattle, where Maddie and Suzanne lived, and worked from their coffee truck, Brewed from the Bean, there had been a coffee festival and cappuccino making competition. But there hadn't been as many entrants as there would be today. The setup, here in the ballroom of one of Seattle's largest hotels, made the contest in Estherville look like the first day of coffee kindergarten.

Suzanne looked around the empty room, then lowered her voice anyway.

"Did you cast a Coffee Vision spell this morning?"

"No." Maddie shook her head. "I didn't want to know what could happen today."

When she was seven, Maddie had stumbled across a crumbling old book called *Wytchcraft for the Chosen* in the local secondhand bookshop.

One spell in particular caught her attention – how to tell someone's future for the next twenty-four hours with the aid of a cup of coffee. When she used her own cup, she caught a glimpse of her future for the next day. When she cast the spell over a customer's cup of coffee, she could peek into their future over the next twenty-four hours.

"I didn't want to know if I won or …" Maddie paused, "… lost."

"I understand." Suzanne touched her arm.

"Where is everyone?" Maddie frowned and checked her watch. "I know we got here early but I didn't think we'd be the first ones to arrive."

"Maybe there was a traffic hold up somewhere." Suzanne wrinkled her snub nose. "We should—"

Before she could finish her sentence, there was a flurry of motion at the ballroom door.

"Am I late?" A tall guy in his late twenties strode into the room. Maddie couldn't wrench her gaze away. He wore a black t-shirt sporting a white badge with the number fourteen, denim jeans – and tattoos. They decorated his muscular, uncovered arms in swirls of green and blue. He also sported a pierced nose and a crew cut. But somehow, his masculine, attractive voice and the good humor in his eyes belied his somewhat tough appearance.

"I don't think so," Maddie answered.

"You're the first person we've seen," Suzanne chimed in, seeming to be equally mesmerized by his arrival. "Apart from the registration clerk outside."

His eyes crinkled with relief. "Good to know." He grinned.

They stood looking at each other for a moment, and then he held out his hand. "I'm Connor."

"I'm Suzanne." She shook his hand. "And this is Maddie."

"Hi," Maddie murmured as she shook his large, calloused hand.

"Are you both competing?" he asked.

"Maddie is," Suzanne replied. "She won the Estherville coffee festival last month."

"It was only a small competition," Maddie put in hastily. She'd been thrilled when she'd won that contest, and the prize had been a trophy and a wild card entry into today's bigger competition, but now she was starting to wonder if she was out of her depth.

"Cool." Connor smiled.

The ballroom door swung open and a stream of people hurried into the room. Maddie's eyes widened as men and women of all ages swarmed toward the espresso stations.

"Everyone!" A tall, slim woman in her forties clapped her hands. Heads turned toward her.

"Now that I have your attention," she barked, "I want everyone to find themselves a station. This competition will start on time. If you are not

competing, go and sit down over there."
She waved a slender hand bedecked with
diamond rings toward the rows of plastic
chairs facing the espresso stations. She
paused, seeming to look at each person in
the room. "If you have not spoken to the
registration clerk outside this room, do so
now. Otherwise you will be disqualified
if you are not wearing a numbered
badge."

"Yikes!" Suzanne whispered to
Maddie. "I hope she's not one of the
judges."

"Me too," Maddie replied, her voice
even lower than her friend's.

The woman who seemed to be in
charge wore her hair in a sleek brunette
bob, and her clothes appeared to be
designer quality, consisting of a tailored
crimson suit with matching kitten heels
decorated with a discreet gold bow on the
heels.

In contrast, Maddie felt a little
inadequate with her brown shoulder-
length hair, lilac shirt and black pants,
and low-heeled shoes.

"We better do what she says," Suzanne said, her natural bounciness subdued. "You find a station and I'll grab a seat."

"I wish Trixie was here," Maddie said wistfully.

"I know." Suzanne smiled sympathetically.

Trixie, Maddie's white and silver Persian, who might also be her familiar, was at home in Estherville. Well, not exactly at home. That morning, Maddie had experienced a whisper of intuition – something that didn't happen *too* often, despite the fact she could cast three spells – and had left Trixie with her mom for the day. And Trixie had not been entirely happy.

Luckily, her mother had promised to look after Trixie, despite not being a cat person, or aware that Maddie was a witch.

"Do you wish Luke was here?" Suzanne asked mischievously.

Maddie blushed, despite her best efforts not to. Luke was Suzanne's brother, whom she'd been dating for the last three and a half weeks. Maddie had been crushing on him for years but it appeared to be only recently that Luke had seemed to return her feelings.

He'd helped her practice for the competition. Maddie reasoned that feeling flustered around him would be good experience for this competition, but unfortunately he'd had a rush order come in to his classic vehicle restoration business, and hadn't been able to make it today. She wasn't sure if that was good or bad news for her nerves.

The staccato sound of someone clapping their hands snagged their attention.

"Find a station right now," the tall slim brunette barked, glaring at Maddie.

Maddie gulped and hurried over to the stations. Most of them had been taken already, but she found one in the second row, next to Connor. He flashed her an encouraging smile as she checked out the espresso machine in front of her.

Everything was supplied for the contestants apart from the coffee beans. Maddie pulled out the beans she usually used in her coffee truck, dark roasted Arabica.

The ballroom door banged and Maddie looked up to see more people trooping in and taking seats in the audience section.

Suzanne met her gaze and gave her a little wave, a smile on her lips. Maddie thought her friend was more excited about today than she was.

"Now that everyone is here—" the tall brunette who seemed to be in charge checked her gold watch "—we can begin. My name is Margot Wheeler. I and the other judges—" she gestured to two men on her left who had come in a few seconds ago, the portly one a little out of breath "—will be sitting over there." She gestured to a long table with three chairs.

"In round one, the first beverage you will make will be an espresso. After we have tasted each one, you'll then go on to make a latte. Then the scores will be tallied, and the finalists will go on to make a mocha in round two, the final round. The overall winner will go on to the nationals, and also win one thousand dollars."

"That grand would really help me out," she heard Connor murmur.

Maddie nodded in understanding. Winning one thousand dollars would be a nice boost to her savings account – or she could put it back into Brewed from the Bean, or share the money with Suzanne, or—

"Don't forget to mention my brand new mocha beverage, MochLava!" A short, blustery man in his sixties made his way importantly to the judges. He snapped his fingers, and a workman wheeled in a silver vat, as tall as Maddie's five foot five.

"I didn't know *that* was going to be here." Margot Wheeler frowned.

"Since I'm the sponsor, I thought it was the perfect opportunity for some publicity," the newcomer said importantly. He took over the microphone after directing the workman to park the vat near the judge's table.

"I'm Fred Beldon," he announced, drawing himself up to his full height of perhaps five foot seven. "The sponsor of today's competition, and I will be the one awarding the check to the winner." He gazed at the competitors as if expecting them to applaud.

After they politely clapped, he motioned to the silver vat. "Feel free to help yourself to a delicious mocha during the break between round one and two." He chuckled. "Tasting MochLava may inspire you to make one almost as good!"

Maddie glanced at the judges, noting their polite smiles. She'd never heard of MochLava before, but her curiosity was aroused. Maybe she would try it, if she managed to get through round one.

"How gauche," a sophisticated looking woman in her thirties on Maddie's other side murmured. She wore what must be a designer suit, in shades of pastel blue and silver which went incredibly well with her blonde hair – the only jarring note the white badge with the number three. If her locks were colored at a salon, it was a skillful job – her hair looked natural and toned well with her fair skin and patrician features. Even her fingernails were nicely-shaped and boasted a French manicure.

Maddie looked at her own fingernails, which were clean, but of different short lengths, and felt a little intimidated by the posh woman's appearance.

"Have you tried that vile stuff?" the elegant woman asked Maddie, her voice just as well-polished as the rest of her.

Maddie shook her head.

"Don't," the woman advised, before turning her attention to the judges.

"Thank you, Fred," Margot, the female judge, said.

"This product will soon be in every coffee house in Seattle," Fred Beldon continued, oblivious to the scowl Margot gave him.

"Not if I have anything to do with it," muttered Connor.

She must really be out of the loop, Maddie thought, risking a glance at Connor – and his tattoos. She'd never heard of this new mocha drink, or Fred Beldon, but both the contestants on either side of her had. Was MochLava a specific Seattle beverage?

"We will now begin," Margot Wheeler stated. The two male judges bobbed their heads in agreement. "You will have four minutes to make three espressos using your own choice of beans. When the buzzer sounds, all coffee making must cease. Does everyone understand?"

Maddie nodded, noticing that all the competitors she could see nodded as well.

"Your time starts now." Margot rang a tinkly bell.

Maddie flew into action. This machine was slightly different to the one she used in her coffee truck, but she'd already taken a few minutes to familiarize herself with it.

The sounds of burring and grinding filled the room, so loud that Maddie knew she should have brought earplugs with her. She peeked to her right at Connor, who had buds of yellow foam sticking out of his ears. He obviously knew what to expect.

Focus.

The machine buzzed and whirred as she pulled a shot of what she hoped was her best espresso ever. The sweet, fruity notes lifted her spirits as she repeated the process twice more.

Maddie concentrated so hard, shutting out all the noise around her, that she startled when a loud buzzer went off. The espressos she'd made looked perfect to her eyes, but she knew it was up to the judges to decide.

All the competitors around her stopped what they were doing when they heard the buzzer.

"Phew," Connor muttered. "That was close."

She looked over at his station, his espresso looking just as good as hers in the tasting glasses.

The judges strolled around the stations, each with a clipboard, trying each espresso and making notes. When they arrived at Maddie's station, Margot, the female judge, ignored her apart from writing down the number on Maddie's badge. She lifted the glass to her lips and tasted the espresso. Was there a hint of pleasure in her expression? Or was it just wishful thinking on Maddie's part?

The two male judges smiled and nodded at her, making notes on their clipboards, then returned to the judge's table.

Maddie sneaked a peek at the posh woman on her left, who seemed satisfied with her performance so far.

"You will now make three lattes," Margot announced, "in five minutes."

The bell sounded again. Rustling on her left alerted her to the fact that her elegant neighbor was using different beans for this beverage. Had Maddie made a mistake by using the same beans for both drinks?

She told herself not to be silly. She'd experimented with various beans during the last three weeks, Luke and Suzanne her willing guinea pigs. She'd even tried out different combinations on her customers, and had kept coming back to her favorite – dark roasted Arabica.

She pushed her doubts to the back of her mind and focused on making the best latte ever.

Buzzzzz.

Maddie's hands fell to her sides as the buzzer sounded. She noticed Connor doing the same, but the sophisticated woman on her left took a few extra seconds to finish pouring her latte. Maddie wondered if the judges would notice.

Once again, she waited for the judges to come to her station. She wished there was a stool she could sit on, as her legs suddenly wobbled. Looking out into the audience, she noticed Suzanne giving her an encouraging smile, and smiled back at her.

At least she could have a break now, before round two – if she scored high enough to compete in that final round. She might even taste the mocha concoction in the silver vat – if she was brave enough.

Margot Wheeler tasted Maddie's latte first, her expression not giving anything away this time. Then the two male judges followed, nodding at her as they set down their glasses. Maddie watched them all write notes on their clipboards, before they turned their attention to her stylish neighbor.

To Maddie's surprise, nothing was said about her competitor taking a few extra seconds to pour her latte after the buzzer sounded. Perhaps there was a little latitude about when to stop making their coffee after the time was up? Or maybe the judges didn't notice. Maddie decided to put it out of her mind. If her neighbor's latte was better than hers, she deserved to get higher marks than Maddie.

"We will now tabulate the scores and post them outside this room in thirty minutes. The semi-finalists will reconvene in two hours for the second round, where you will make three mochas," Margot announced, checking her watch.

"Phew," Connor murmured to her as he put a packet of coffee beans back into his satchel. "I could do with a break after that."

"I know what you mean," Maddie said. Now that the intensity of the competition was over for the moment, all she wanted to do was flop into a chair and relax – until it was time for the next round.

"How do you think you went?" Suzanne rushed over to her. A few other members of the audience headed toward the stations to chat with her fellow competitors.

"I don't know." Maddie scrunched her nose. "I think I did okay but—"

"You looked awesome up there," Suzanne assured her with a grin. "I can't wait until they reveal the scores." She turned to Connor. "What was that about the mocha drink – MochLava?" She gestured to the silver vat near the judge's table. The three judges seemed deep in discussion, Margot pointing at her clipboard with a crimson fingernail.

"It's a new coffee beverage, mass produced in a factory in Seattle." Connor grimaced. "Fred Beldon doesn't have a clue about coffee – or chocolate – but he thinks he does. And he thinks he's going to get rich with that swill."

"I guess you've tasted it then?" Suzanne asked.

"Yeah. He visited a lot of the coffee shops offering samples. My boss thought it might be good for business, and we all tried it." His face split into a grin. "And it was so bad, my boss told us never to speak about it again."

"If it's so terrible, why is he sponsoring the competition?" Maddie asked.

Connor shrugged. "Money talks, I guess. And if there wasn't a sponsor, the competition mightn't have gone ahead or offered a prize."

"One thousand dollars is an attractive sum," Suzanne mused, "along with an entry into the nationals."

"Yeah," Connor agreed. "And like I told Maddie, I could really use the money right now. But it depends if my coffee is the best today." He turned to Maddie. "You looked like you knew what you were doing."

"Thanks." She smiled shyly. "Suzanne and I operate a coffee truck in Estherville."

"It's one hundred miles from Seattle," Suzanne put in helpfully. "Maddie makes the coffee, and I'm in charge of the register and making goodies like health balls. Where do you work?"

Maddie hoped Connor didn't mind the inquisitive question.

"In a hipster coffee shop not far from here. I'm lucky my boss knows his coffee beans, though." He lowered his voice. "I've heard some coffee shops have decided to carry the MochLava because the owners will do practically anything to improve their bottom line – but they don't realize just how bad the stuff is."

"Now you've got me curious." Suzanne's eyes sparkled.

"Taste it and see for yourself." He motioned to the silver vat.

"Come on, Mads." Suzanne's strawberry-blonde ponytail bounced as she headed over to the vat.

"Don't say I didn't warn you," Connor chuckled as Maddie passed him.

There were paper cups next to the bubbling vat as well as a long-handled silver spoon.

Suzanne ladled a large spoonful into a cup, then handed it to Maddie. "Drink up."

"You first." Maddie doubtfully eyed the liquid concoction. It didn't smell like good coffee – or chocolate – should. But she had to admit, she was a little curious.

"Ready?" Suzanne held up her own cup, and gently tapped it against Maddie's.

"Okay." Maddie took a tentative sip, her eyes widening as the mocha slid down her throat.

Yuck.

Suzanne swallowed, then blinked. "I don't know if this is better or worse than one of Claudine's mochas."

Maddie stifled a giggle. Claudine was their nemesis and owned a coffee shop in Estherville. She was always stopping by their coffee truck and making snarky comments, while Maddie and Suzanne wondered how she stayed in business with her terrible coffee and curmudgeonly personality.

Luckily, there was a trashcan next to the mocha vat and they dumped their semi-full cups into the receptacle.

"Is it that bad?" A soft voice asked from behind them.

"Yep," Suzanne admitted cheerfully as they both turned around.

A slim girl who appeared to be in her early twenties blushed under their scrutiny, as if surprised at her own courage at asking the question. Maddie recognized her as a fellow competitor – she'd had one of the stations at the back of the room.

"Want some?" Suzanne held out the ladle to her.

"Oh no." The girl shook her head. "I believe you." She reminded Maddie of a startled deer.

"I'm Maddie." Maddie smiled gently.

"And I'm Suzanne," Suzanne chimed in. "Maddie's the one competing and I was in the audience."

"I'm Ellie," the shy girl replied.

"I love your earrings," Maddie said, leaning forward as she admired them. Small pink and gold fairies dangled from the girl's ears, and combined with her white blonde hair complete with wispy bangs, she could almost pass as a fairy herself. Somehow, Maddie suspected her hair was that shade naturally, not skillfully applied in a salon.

"Thanks." Ellie looked pleased at the compliment. "My little sister said I should wear them for luck."

"How do you think you've done so far?" Suzanne asked curiously.

"I don't know." Ellie shrugged. "I didn't think there would be so many competitors here, but my boss said I should enter."

"What sort of beans did you use?" Now it was Maddie's turn to be inquisitive. She knew that to be a competitor today, you had to have won a barista competition, and be somewhat experienced.

"An Ethiopian blend," Ellie replied. "I love the mellow sweetness and—"

"Ethiopian is one of my favorites." Connor appeared.

"Really?" Ellie looked surprised.

"Yeah." Connor smiled at her. "I'm Connor." He held out a hand to Ellie.

After a second's hesitation, Ellie shook his hand. "Ellie."

"Where do you work?" Connor asked.

"At Hannon's," Ellie replied. "You probably haven't heard of it – it's just a small place." She seemed to have trouble taking her eyes off his muscular tattooed arms and his nose piercing.

"Are you serious? I go there all the time when I'm tired of making coffee for myself." He furrowed his brow. "I haven't seen you there, though."

"I haven't seen you there, either." Ellie blushed as if she thought she was being too forward. "But I'm usually in the back, making the orders."

"Yeah." Connor nodded. "The way that place is set up, you'd have a hard time seeing the barista. Where I work is different – the boss wants all the hipsters – and wannabes – to see the coffee being made in front of them."

"What …" Ellie swallowed. "What's your favorite drink at Hannon's?"

"A long macchiato topped up."

Ellie's eyes widened. "Were you there yesterday afternoon? At four o'clock?"

"Yeah." He grinned.

"You're *him*. Not many people ask for that specific drink."

"You made my coffee yesterday?"

Ellie nodded.

Maddie wondered if she and Suzanne should give them some time alone. It looked like a potential romance was brewing.

But before she could tactfully withdraw, a man in his forties with dark brown hair and a grumpy expression on his face came up to them. He wore a gray shirt with mid-blue buttons rimmed in gold, and black trousers.

"How much longer do you think they'll take to tabulate the scores?" He jerked his head toward the judge's table, where the three judges appeared to still be discussing the results of round one.

Connor dragged his eyes away from Ellie and looked at his chunky functional watch. "Probably not too much longer, Brad."

"I hope not," the newcomer muttered. He cast a distasteful glance toward the vat of mocha. "Have any of you tried that – slop?"

"Yep." Suzanne shuddered dramatically.

Maddie nodded.

"More fool you," he replied. "Everyone who appreciates coffee in this city knows not to touch Fred Beldon's stuff." He eyed Maddie and Suzanne skeptically. "I guess you two aren't from around here."

"We're from Estherville," Maddie replied.

"Where?" He frowned.

"Estherville," Suzanne said loudly, as if he were hard of hearing. "It's one hundred miles away."

"Oh. That explains it." His brow cleared, as if immediately dismissing them from contention.

Maddie was taken aback by his rudeness. So far, everyone she had met had seemed friendly – even the elegant competitor at the next station to her hadn't been rude like this man. Everyone apart from the judge, Margot Wheeler …

"So how do you think you did?" Connor filled in the silence as he addressed the other man.

"I should get into the second round, no problem," Brad replied. "This isn't my first competition, that's for sure. And—" he tapped his second top button which was a darker blue than the others "—I'm wearing my lucky shirt." He smirked. "How about you?"

"I hope I make it to the second round," Connor replied, "but I think there's some stiff competition today." He glanced at Maddie and then at Ellie, his gaze lingering on her.

"As long as the judges are fair, I shouldn't have a problem," Brad continued, a swift scowl marring his face as he glanced at the judge's table.

Maddie blinked, not sure if she saw the frown or not.

"Look." Suzanne nudged her.

Maddie followed her gaze. The three judges got up from the table and headed toward the entrance.

"Do you think they're going to post the scores now?" Suzanne asked hopefully.

Maddie watched as Margot Wheeler pulled off a large sheet of paper from her clipboard as she walked out of the room.

"Maybe," Maddie replied, not sure if she wanted to know what her score was. What if she didn't make it to round two? She and Suzanne had closed the coffee truck today in order to make it to Seattle in time. What if all her weeks of preparation – and nerves – had been in vain?

But spending time with Suzanne – and Luke – would never be a waste of time. And Trixie had seemed interested in the practice sessions, too. The memory of Trixie's pouting today when Maddie had dropped her off at her mom's place on the way to Seattle flashed through her mind. It had definitely been a pout, despite Trixie being a cat, not a human.

"Maybe we should go and check it out," Connor suggested.

"Good idea." Suzanne smiled, flicking a glance toward the door the judges had just exited.

Ellie nodded.

"Sure. Why not?" Brad agreed.

They trooped through the door. Tacked up on the wall was a list of names.

Maddie's heart accelerated. Now she would find out if she'd made it through to round two.

"Yes!" Connor sounded gratified. "And look," she heard him say to Ellie, "you're in round two as well."

"Go and see." Suzanne nudged her.

The others made room for Maddie to study the scores. Each contestant's name, their badge number, and their scores were posted in order from the highest rank to the lowest. The competitors who had made it through to round two were highlighted at the top of the page.

Maddie Goodwell. Round Two.

Her heart stuttered and she blinked, making sure she hadn't misread the chart.

She'd made it to the next round – and right now she was in third place overall!

Out of the three scores for her espresso and again for her latte, only one judge had marked her quite low. But the high marks from the other two judges had propelled her to the second round.

Her gaze drifted down the sheet, and she noticed that everyone seemed to have low marks awarded to them for both drinks, from Margot Wheeler. The scores from the other two judges were higher for everyone else, too.

Except … her elegant neighbor, who had worn the badge with the number three on her blue and silver designer outfit, did not have such low marks from Margot Wheeler. Overall, her score was only one point lower than Maddie's but the difference between her two high scores and one low score wasn't as noticeable – her high scores weren't as high as Maddie's but her low score wasn't as low as Maddie's.

Maddie frowned at the anomaly – did it mean anything?

"Just as well," she heard Brad growl behind her. He sounded as if he were grinding his teeth. "But there's no way I should be in eighth place."

Her eyes scanned the scores once more. His badge number was twenty, and she saw that Brad had made the last spot for round two.

"Oh, good." The elegant woman who had been her neighbor during round one, glided up.

Maddie stepped aside so she would have plenty of room to study the scores, although Maddie knew she'd placed fourth.

"Yes, I thought so," the elegant woman continued, a small smile touching her lips. She turned to Maddie. "How did you do?"

Maddie pointed to her name above her neighbor's. "I made it to the second round."

The sophisticated woman looked surprised for an instant, then smiled. "Congratulations. I see I just came in after you." She gestured to the badge marked with a three on her lapel, then held out her hand. "I'm Diana Swift."

"I'm Maddie," she replied, shaking the other woman's hand.

"Do you work as a barista?" Diana Swift asked curiously.

"Yes," Maddie replied. "My friend and I run a coffee truck in Estherville, one hundred miles away."

"That sounds very enterprising," Diana Swift responded. "I only entered this competition as a way to get into the nationals. I'm starting my own chain of coffee shops, and the flagship store will be right here in Seattle."

"Wow," Maddie murmured, admiring the other woman's ambition. She and Suzanne had spoken about expanding with another truck, but had decided the time wasn't right yet. Diana Swift only looked around five to ten years older than Maddie.

"I have the finance in place and yesterday I signed the lease for the first store," Diana Swift continued. "But a spot in the nationals will instantly give me credibility and will be a great selling point to customers."

Maddie nodded. She'd been so focused on practicing – and alternately being flustered and enjoying Luke's company in her coffee making sessions – that she hadn't really thought that far ahead. She'd just concentrated on her performance today.

Besides, there was the whole matter that she might be a witch. Ever since she had turned twenty-seven a couple of months ago, the book she'd bought as a child, *Wytchcraft for the Chosen,* had predicted that a witch came into her full powers at that age. So far, that hadn't happened. But with every full moon after that birthday, she'd discovered the ability to cast a new spell.

Now, she was able to cast the Tell the Truth spell and the Escape your Enemy spell.

The next full moon was in two days' time …

"That sounds very impressive," Suzanne grinned as she joined them. "Hi, I'm Suzanne, Maddie's friend and business partner." She shook hands with Diana Swift. "I'd love to visit your coffee shop when you open."

"I'll invite you both to the grand opening," Diana promised. "Do you have a business card?"

Maddie and Suzanne looked at each other.

"Not yet," Suzanne replied. "But we will."

Maddie didn't think they needed a business card in Estherville, where a lot of people knew who they were and the quality of the coffee they served. Since they were parked in the same spot six days per week, at the town square, their truck was easy to find.

"A business card is essential if you want to be taken seriously," Diana Swift told Suzanne. "Here, take one of mine." She plucked a white and silver card from her designer purse. "Call me early next month. I should have the exact date of the opening by then."

"I will," Suzanne promised, placing the card in her purse. "Thank you."

"I'll see you in round two, Maddie." Diana smiled, then headed down the hall to the main section of the hotel.

"I'm starving," Suzanne declared. "Let's get something to eat."

"I don't think I could manage anything right now," Maddie protested, her stomach clenching at the thought of having to compete in round two. *At least she'd made it this far.* "But I'd love to sit down for a while."

"Then let's go." Suzanne's ponytail bobbed as she set off. "I spotted a café near the elevators." She looked at her watch. "We've got over an hour before you have to get back here for the next round."

Maddie followed her friend, hoping the café wouldn't be too crowded. Luckily, there were a couple of tables vacant, and Maddie sat down in a steel chair as Suzanne scanned the menu.

A low hum of conversation filled the space, punctuated with the occasional clatter of cutlery.

"Are you sure you don't want anything?" Suzanne asked, waving the menu toward Maddie.

"Just a glass of water," Maddie replied. Although she loved drinking coffee as well as making it, she didn't think she needed any caffeine right now, even though the floral scent of coffee beans wafted through the space.

"Oh, look," Suzanne whispered, staring at a corner of the café.

Maddie followed her gaze.

"Isn't that Fred Beldon, who's sponsoring the competition?" Suzanne's voice was hushed.

"Yes," Maddie replied in a low voice.

"I wonder what he's doing here?"

"Getting something to eat?" Maddie could see that the blustery man had a big plate of food in front of him.

"Does he really think his mocha drink is going to take off?" Suzanne crinkled her brow. "It tasted pretty bad."

"I know." Maddie nodded. "But if he has the right connections …"

"And enough money," Suzanne added. "Look at Diana Swift. She's opening a chain of coffee shops but you've beaten her in the competition."

"So far," Maddie said cautiously. "There's still round two."

"And you've got a great chance of winning," Suzanne said encouragingly. "You're coming third right now." Her eyes glinted with curiosity. "Do you know who's in front of you?"

"Ellie is coming first, and then Connor," she replied, a smile on her lips.

"No way!" Suzanne giggled. "That's awesome, except it's not you in first place. Do you think they'll—" she glanced around and lowered her voice, although none of the other customers seemed interested in their conversation "—get together?"

"Who knows?" Maddie replied diplomatically, although she was secretly hoping they would. The combination of the big tough guy – although his appearance seemed to belie his personality – with the delicate looking Ellie mightn't seem to be a good match at first, but Maddie remembered the way the two of them had looked at each other when they'd realized that Ellie had been making Connor's coffee – for how long? Weeks? Months? Even years? It was like a fairytale romance.

Once again Maddie remembered the fairy earrings Ellie wore. Was there magic involved with the two of them meeting?

She shook her head as if to clear it. Although she was limited proof that magic and witches existed – even familiars – she didn't know if fairies were real or not.

"We should get back." Suzanne interrupted her musing after finishing her hazelnut latte and slice of banana bread.

Maddie had been so wrapped up in her thoughts, her friend's voice gave her a start.

"How was the coffee?" She gestured to the empty glass.

"Not as good as yours." Suzanne grinned. "But it wasn't bad. A lot better than that mocha drink." She tilted her head, indicating Fred, eating at his table in the corner.

On the way back to the ballroom, Maddie checked her watch. Fifteen minutes before round two started. She told herself to relax as she and Suzanne walked down the hallway, but it was no good. She was too keyed up again to do anything apart from forcing her feet in the direction of the ballroom.

A scream made Maddie freeze, one foot in mid-air. She turned to Suzanne, her eyes wide.

Before she could say anything, another scream rent the air.

"It's coming from the ballroom." Suzanne grabbed her hand and pulled her toward the noise.

They ran to the ballroom, Maddie hoping they wouldn't come across something awful. Maybe someone had fallen down. Or stubbed their toe.

But she had a sinking suspicion in the pit of her stomach that it *was* something awful.

As they reached the ballroom door, Diana Swift rushed out, her eyes wild. "She's dead!"

CHAPTER 2

"Wait!" Maddie called out as the elegant woman raced down the hallway, back toward the main area of the hotel.

But Diana ignored her and kept running.

Suzanne turned to Maddie. "Do you think we should go in there?"

"No." Maddie hesitated. "But what if whoever is in there isn't dead and needs help? If we don't go in and see—"

"Then they could very well die." Suzanne nodded. "We better go in."

They stood staring at the now closed door.

"On three." Maddie drew a deep breath.

"One," Suzanne counted.

"Two," Maddie said.

"Three." They pushed open the door and strode inside.

At first glance, Maddie didn't see anything out of the ordinary. Her gaze flickered over the espresso stations. Everything looked fine.

She and Suzanne viewed the rows of plastic chairs for the audience – no one was slumped over – in fact nobody occupied that part of the room.

And then …

A pair of legs, ending in crimson shoes decorated with a discreet gold bow on each heel, dangled from the mocha vat.

"Suzanne." Maddie's voice was a strangled whisper. "Over there."

"Where – oh!" Suzanne's mouth froze in a perfect O.

Maddie raced to the vat. What if Margot Wheeler wasn't dead? If there was a possibility that the woman was still alive, then she and Suzanne had to help her.

Margot's head and torso were submerged in the vat of bubbling mocha.

"Help me get her out," Maddie urged.

Before Suzanne could do anything, a loud voice sounded:

"Stop right there!"

Maddie turned. A hotel security guard hurried into the room, accompanied by Diana.

The guard was middle-aged, with a paunch and slicked back dark hair.

"Get away from the body," he barked.

"I was trying to help her." Maddie slowly took a step away from the vat. "Maybe she's not dead."

"I'm calling for backup." The guard spoke into his radio, squawks emitting from it.

"But if Maddie's right, and she isn't dead?" Suzanne spoke up over the radio static.

"Ah, jeez." After a second's hesitation, the guard heaved Margot out of the vat and squatted down beside her.

Cocoa brown liquid covered Margot's face and dribbled down her neck and chest, staining her crimson suit.

"I told you she was dead," Diana spoke, staring at the female judge. "I don't think CPR is going to help her."

"How do you know this?" the guard asked sharply. He looked at the three of them. "All of you, stay where you are."

"You don't think I had something to do with this, do you?" demanded Diana, paling. "I was the one who sought help."

Before the guard could reply, two more security guards rushed in, joining their colleague.

"I've already called the police," one of them said. "We need to secure the scene until they get here."

"Then make sure those three don't leave." The paunchy security guard pointed to Maddie, Suzanne, and Diana. "They might have had something to do with it."

Maddie bit her lip at the accusation. Suzanne huffed and looked daggers at the man, and Diana pursed her mouth.

Maddie watched one of the security guards attempt CPR, but it looked like it was hopeless.

The door swung open and Ellie and Connor entered, talking and laughing. They stopped abruptly as they took in the scene.

"What … what happened?" Ellie asked in a tiny whisper.

Connor looked shocked.

"It appears that Margot Wheeler is dead." Suzanne hurried over to them, Maddie right behind her.

"No talking and no moving," snapped the paunchy security guard who'd first appeared in the ballroom.

Ellie looked like she wanted to run out of there, despite being ordered not to. Connor put his arm around her in a comforting gesture.

"Isn't anyone guarding the door?" the second guard asked.

The third guard stopped the chest compressions, shaking his head and looking dejected.

Maddie's knees wobbled. Margot hadn't seemed like the friendliest person this morning, but that didn't mean she deserved to be killed.

Was it an accident?

Or murder?

The ballroom door opened again, and this time a man in his thirties dressed in plain clothes, flanked by two uniformed police officers, entered the room. He strode over to the security guards, and after talking briefly with them, and taking some photos on his phone, addressed the rest of the room.

"I'm Detective Rawson," he began. "None of you are to leave the room until I've spoken with each of you." His russet hair and strong-chinned face with a hint of stubble suggested arguing with him was a bad idea.

Brad barged into the room, stopping in his tracks as he took in the tableau.

"What's going on?" He looked shocked.

"It appears a woman has been the victim of foul play," the detective answered. "And you are?"

"Brad Dawes," he replied. "A round two finalist."

More people suddenly appeared at the door. Perhaps they'd watched round one from the audience, and were back for round two of the competition. Maddie didn't recognize them as competitors.

Detective Rawson jerked his head and a police officer hurried over to the door, barring the crowd from entering.

"Who was the first person to find the victim?" the detective asked, looking hard at Maddie, Suzanne, and the rest of the contestants in the room.

"I was," Diana admitted.

"But when I got here, these two—" the paunchy security guard who'd arrived first indicated Maddie and Suzanne "— were next to the body."

"Is this true?" Detective Rawson asked Maddie and Suzanne, a frown marring his features. "What were you doing?"

"She was in the mocha vat when I found her," Diana interrupted.

Maddie and Suzanne nodded vigorously.

"That's right." Maddie found her voice, wishing the detective's penetrating gaze didn't seem to be piercing through to her core. If he looked at criminals like that, he must get a lot of confessions. She felt like confessing to something but she couldn't think of anything – apart from the fact that she might be a witch, and she had never told anyone that, except Suzanne.

"Yes," Suzanne agreed. "We were about to try and lift her out of the vat when the security guard came in." She pointed to the guard who'd been first on the scene.

"All right." The detective sighed. "Let me get this straight. You are all here today for a barista competition, is that correct?"

"Yes," Brad responded, looking at his watch. "And the second round was supposed to start in four minutes."

Maddie felt a little rumpled after round one, but Brad looked fresh and unwrinkled, as if competing in a barista competition was no big deal. Perhaps it wasn't – for him. After all, he'd said this wasn't his first time competing, and he wore his "lucky" shirt.

"Well, it won't be happening any time soon," the detective told him.

"What do you mean?" Brad narrowed his eyes.

"I mean—" Detective Rawson gestured to the victim, "we need to secure the crime scene – what's left of it, anyway – and get everyone's statement. That's going to take some time. And we need to identify the victim."

They were ushered out of the ballroom, Detective Rawson instructing the officers to seal the crime scene. Maddie and Suzanne, along with the others, followed the detective next door, to a smaller room.

"Okay," Detective Rawson said, looking at Maddie, Suzanne and Diana. "Do you know who the victim was?"

"Margot Wheeler," Diana told the detective. "She was one of the judges."

The detective whipped out a fancy notebook and gold pen and jotted down something.

"Did anyone have any dealings with her before today?" he asked.

Maddie and Suzanne shook their heads. Maddie noticed that Diana hesitated, then shook her head as well.

"No," Ellie replied in a whisper.

"No," Connor said firmly, his arm still around Ellie's shoulders.

"No," Brad replied.

"And the six of you made it through to round two?" Detective Rawson asked.

"No," Suzanne replied. "Maddie made it to the second round and I was watching the first round from the audience. But the rest of them made it to round two, I believe." She gestured to Maddie and the other four.

"There should be another three finalists somewhere," Brad said, looking around the room as if expecting them to pop up from behind the espresso stations. "Eight made it through to round two, which is also the final round."

"They might be outside, and I'll speak to them later," Detective Rawson informed him. "Now, how did the judge seem this morning?"

"Bossy," Suzanne murmured under her breath.

"And you are?" the detective enquired, pinning Suzanne with a steely-eyed stare.

"Suzanne Taylor," she replied. "And she was bossy." Her voice was louder. "At least I thought so, but I wasn't competing."

"She seemed to be in charge," Maddie contributed, not wanting her friend to get into trouble.

"That's right," Connor agreed. "She was the judge who told us what was going to happen today."

"Apart from the fact she was going to be murdered," Brad muttered.

"And she marked everyone pretty low," Connor said.

"What do you mean?" The detective stared at the muscular, tattooed guy.

Connor shrugged. "The scores were posted outside, and she seemed to give everyone low marks – much lower than the other two judges, apart from one person." His gaze zoomed past Maddie until it landed on Diana.

"She marked me low as well," the elegant woman protested.

"But not as low as everyone else," Suzanne blurted out.

"That's right," Brad agreed with a scowl.

Diana's expression flashed with indignation. "If that's true, then why would I kill her? Perhaps it was one of you." Her hand swept in the direction of Maddie and the other suspects.

Before anyone could utter a word, Detective Rawson took charge.

"I'll speak with you individually now," he said, "starting with you." He pointed to Maddie.

Maddie gulped. Suzanne squeezed her hand before she followed the detective to the other side of the room.

Maddie gave Detective Rawson her name and address, then told him she'd won the small Estherville coffee festival last month which gave her the wildcard entry into today's competition.

"So, how are you doing so far?" he asked.

"I'm coming third right now," Maddie replied, wondering at his question. He'd be able to see from the rankings posted outside the room where each competitor was placed.

"Congratulations. Now, Estherville." He looked down at his notes. "I have an uncle who works there. For the sheriff's department."

"You do?" Maddie furrowed her brow.

"Detective Edgewater."

"Oh, I know him." Maddie smiled before realizing that perhaps she'd just said the wrong thing.

"You do?" He looked at her keenly. "How?"

She hesitated, then decided to be truthful. "I met him for the first time when one of my customers died." Should she mention the incident at Estherville's coffee festival last month? Before she could decide, he continued the questioning.

"What sort of business do you run?"

"Suzanne and I operate Brewed from the Bean. It's a coffee truck," she told him. "We're at the town square in Estherville."

She watched make some notes.

"And why was that vat of mocha in the other room?"

"I don't know much about it," she told him. "Apparently it's something to do with the sponsor of this competition – Fred Beldon. He said his mocha drink – MochLava – will be in Seattle cafés soon, and—" she paused. Should she tell the detective the other contestants' views on the subject?

"And?" he prodded. "Go on."

"Some of the contestants didn't seem to like the beverage," she said in a rush. "Suzanne and I tried it after round one and it was horrible." She tried not to screw up her face at the memory.

"When was the last time you saw Margot Wheeler alive?" he asked.

"When she went outside to post the scores," Maddie answered. "Suzanne and I went to take a look, but I didn't notice Margot in the hallway."

After Maddie told him that she and Suzanne went to the hotel coffee shop, she remembered who they'd seen there.

"Fred Beldon was there in the café, at a table by himself," she told the detective. "Then Suzanne and I came back here. We heard Diana scream as we neared the ballroom, and then she rushed out, saying, "She's dead." Suzanne and I went inside to check and then that's when the first security guard showed up."

Maddie paused. "Did Margot drown in the mocha vat?"

"That's what it looks like," the detective informed her. "We'll know more after the autopsy."

She shuddered. What a terrible way to die. She'd suspected that might have been the case, but now it was semi-official, the horror of what had happened to the female judge swept over her.

"Thanks, Ms. Goodwell." The detective finished writing in his notebook. "I'll need to get a formal statement from you later so stay outside in the hallway until I tell you that you can leave."

"Yes, sir," Maddie replied, wishing she and Suzanne could leave right now and drive back to Estherville. All she wanted to do was to relax with her best friend and snuggle with Trixie. Thank goodness she'd left the Persian with Mom.

Maddie walked toward door leading to the hallway, glad the interview was over.

"How was it?" Suzanne asked her, just as the detective gestured for her to head toward him for her turn to be grilled.

Maddie watched her friend go, noticing that Suzanne's ponytail seemed subdued for once, just like the rest of her.

Afterward, when Suzanne met Maddie in the hall, she asked, "Did he tell you he's Detective Edgewater's nephew?"

"Yes." Maddie nodded. "I don't know if that's good news or bad."

"It's good if he asks his uncle about us. Detective Edgewater will vouch for us."

"I hope so," Maddie replied, thinking that their exposure to two dead bodies in sleepy Estherville wasn't exactly a ringing endorsement.

"I wonder," Suzanne mused, "if—"

"My MochLava!" Fred Beldon appeared in the hallway, his big belly jiggling under his suit. "What happened?"

"Stop right there, sir." One of the uniformed police officers headed off Fred before he could enter the ballroom.

"No one is supposed to enter that room." Detective Rawson stuck his head out of the temporary interviewing room and frowned at the police officer.

"I'm sorry, sir, he took us by surprise," the officer replied.

"I'll deal with this gentleman next." The detective indicated the mocha sponsor.

"What's happened?" Fred looked distressed.

"There's been an incident." The detective guided him inside the small room, indicating to Connor that his interview was over for now.

Maddie watched the detective talk to Fred before he closed the door, and the expressions flitting across the big man's face – shock and horror – as she guessed the detective apprised him of the female judge's fate.

"I wish we could get out of here." Suzanne nudged her. "All I want to do is go home."

"Me too," Maddie replied, heartfelt.

"Do you think *he* did it?" Suzanne looked at the now closed door of the temporary interview room.

"Fred? No – why? Do you think he killed the judge?" Maddie kept her voice low.

"I don't know." Suzanne scrunched up her nose. "But she didn't seem to be a fan of his mocha drink."

"I don't think anyone was," Maddie replied. "We weren't."

"Yeah, it was horrible." Suzanne grimaced. "But maybe Fred didn't appreciate the fact that she didn't like it. Maybe she was going to do something about it."

"Like what? Stop him from selling it to cafes in Seattle?" Maddie eyed her friend skeptically. "How would she do that?"

"I don't know," Suzanne admitted. "But I don't see how this could be an accident. Someone drowned Margot and right now we're all suspects."

CHAPTER 3

One hour later, Maddie wriggled on the hard plastic chair that the officers had eventually provided in the hallway, trying to get comfortable.

"How much longer?" Suzanne asked, twisting around in her seat.

The two male judges had been interviewed, as well as the remaining finalists. Now, everyone sat down, talking amongst themselves, while the detective spoke to the uniformed police officers.

"Can I have everyone's attention," Detective Rawson called out. "The rest of today's competition will be postponed."

Some of the finalists groaned, looking disappointed. Brad looked annoyed and fiddled with one of the gold-rimmed buttons on his shirt.

"I've just gotten word that the rest of the hotel's conference rooms are fully booked for the weekend. And I've been told that three judges are needed for round two." He looked over at the two male judges in confirmation.

The finalists muttered to each other. Maddie looked expectantly at Suzanne. Did this mean they could go home?

The portly male judge rose and addressed the finalists.

"I've just spoken to hotel management and we will be able to hold round two next weekend. I realize some of you may need to adjust your schedules in order to compete next Saturday, and I apologize but—" he swallowed hard "—I'm sure none of us expected this to happen, especially Margot Wheeler."

There were murmurs of agreement from the small crowd.

Maddie noticed Ellie looked dismayed, while Connor exhaled heavily, as they sat together.

Diana Swift looked regretful – but Maddie wasn't sure if it was because of the postponement of the competition, or the fact that a woman had died today.

Detective Rawson took over. "I'm going to have to request that anyone who is from out of town stay here tonight while the scene is processed. I'll need full statements from everyone. The hotel has been able to provide accommodation for everyone who needs to stay here. And," he added, seeming to assess each person individually with a sharp glance, "no one is to leave this hotel until I say so, even if you do live in Seattle. Is that clear?"

There was a murmur of reluctant assent.

"Does he really think someone here killed Margot?" Suzanne murmured to Maddie.

"I think so," she replied softly, not wanting to catch the detective's attention.

Maddie and Suzanne were escorted to a room on the fifth floor of the hotel. Maddie had filled in an entry form in order to compete and had been required to disclose her address. She wondered if any of the other competitors were out of town and if so, if she and Suzanne would run into them later.

"Not bad," Suzanne approved as they walked into the twin room. Two queen size beds with pastel blue bedspreads, matching blue carpet, and cream drapes created a soothing décor. A TV sat opposite the beds, and a mahogany table and four matching chairs, as well as an armoire, completed the furnishings.

"If you give me your cell phone numbers, we'll call when you're required to give full statements," the uniformed police officer told them.

Once Maddie and Suzanne had done so, the officer departed, reminding them not to leave the hotel grounds until given permission.

"Let's check out the bathroom," Suzanne said, heading toward the door near the armoire.

Maddie followed, a smile touching her lips as she took in the big bathtub, shower cubicle complete with jet spray, double vanity, and gleaming white toilet.

"Wow." After the events of today, she looked forward to soaking in that tub tonight. There was even a bottle of hotel branded bubble bath sitting next to the silver bath taps.

"I know," Suzanne agreed. "If we ever want to stay the night again in Seattle, we must remember this place."

"If only Margot hadn't had to die," Maddie said regretfully.

"Yeah." Suzanne looked uncomfortable.

"I'm just glad Trixie is staying with Mom today. Oh! I better call her and let her know we won't be coming home tonight."

Maddie used her cell phone to call her mother. She and Trixie hadn't been apart for a night before – would Trixie be okay?

Her mother reassured her that Trixie was being "very good" and it was no trouble to keep her overnight. Luckily, Maddie had taken the Persian's water bowl and plenty of her favorite food, as well as her litter tray to her mother's house that morning. She just hoped the feline would understand why Maddie wasn't coming home tonight.

"Everything okay?" Suzanne asked when Maddie ended the call.

"Yes. But I didn't know how Mom would react if I asked to speak to Trixie on the phone."

"That would have been fun." Suzanne giggled.

"Uh-huh." Maddie smiled. She was sure if she'd spoken to Trixie on the

phone, the cat would have understood –
after all, Maddie was pretty sure now that
Trixie was her familiar. But since
Maddie's parents didn't know anything
about the ancient magic book, *Wytchcraft
for the Chosen*, or the fact that Maddie
had three spells under her belt, she
thought her mom might have wondered
exactly why Maddie wanted to speak to
her cat on the phone.

"Maybe you could communicate with
Trixie telepathically." Suzanne snapped
her fingers. "Didn't you say that's what
she did with you last month?"

"Yes."

"And then maybe you better cast a
Coffee Vision spell, to give us a clue
about what's going to happen in the next
twenty-four hours."

"One thing at a time," Maddie
protested. She sank onto one of the beds,
the firm yet comfy mattress making her
want to lie down and let the events of
today wash over her. But she couldn't –
not yet, anyway.

Exhaling, she closed her eyes and
pictured Trixie. Her white, fluffy fur, her
silver plumy tail, and her unusual

turquoise eyes. She'd never attempted to do this before, but Suzanne was right – there was no harm in seeing if she could talk to her cat telepathically.

Maddie imagined cuddling Trixie, stroking her fur, then pictured her sitting on the sofa at home, guarding *Wytchcraft for the Chosen*, something she seemed to enjoy doing.

Suddenly, an image flashed before her eyes of Trixie at her mother's house, sitting in an armchair and dozing.

Trixie, she called mentally. The Persian blinked her eyes open and slowly sat up.

It was working! Surely it was working, or else Maddie was imagining the whole thing.

Suzanne and I have to stay in Seattle overnight, but I'll be home as soon as possible tomorrow. Mom will look after you until then.

"Mrrow," Trixie replied, then she yawned, her pink tongue darting out. She gave a long blink, as if letting Maddie know everything was okay, then settled back down in the chair, preparing to doze off again.

Maddie smiled at the image, then slowly opened her eyes, giving herself a few seconds to adjust to fully being back in the hotel room.

"Well?" Suzanne asked eagerly. "Did it work? What did Trixie say?"

Maddie laughed. "She didn't say anything except "Mrrow." But she seems okay. And she didn't seem fazed at all that we were communicating like that." She hesitated. "Unless I imagined the whole thing."

"I'm sure you didn't," Suzanne said stoutly. "Why shouldn't you and Trixie be able to talk to each other that way? You're both witchy." She sighed. "I wish I was."

"Maybe one day there'll be a spell in the book that can give you magical powers – if that's what you want," Maddie replied.

Since she'd turned twenty-seven – or seven-and-twenty as *Wytchcraft for the Chosen* stated, she had come across spells she didn't remember seeing in the ancient tome before. And since she'd had the book for twenty years, it was something that surprised her.

Last month, she'd wondered if receiving her full powers meant having the ability to cast one unique spell per month – at that rate, it would take her eight years – plenty of time to discover lots of new spells.

"That would be so awesome!" Suzanne grinned.

Just then, Maddie's cell phone rang. *Brring brring.* She answered, surprised to hear the detective's authoritative voice.

"Who was it?" Suzanne asked when Maddie ended the call.

"Detective Rawson. He wants to see both of us now."

"Down at the ballroom?" Suzanne asked.

Maddie shook her head. "They've found a small room they can use instead. It's near the coffee shop."

"Maybe we can get something to eat afterward." Suzanne checked her watch. "I can't believe it's five p.m. already!"

"Me neither," Maddie agreed as they trooped out of the hotel room.

They took the elevator to the lobby and made their way to the coffee shop.

Opposite was a small room with a uniformed police officer standing outside.

"That must be it." Suzanne nudged her.

Detective Rawson took Maddie's statement first, then she waited outside while he took Suzanne's, conscious the whole time of the police officer's assessing gaze. Did he really think she'd murdered Margot? Did the detective? Surely they had stronger suspects to consider than the two of them.

Besides, her full statement was practically the same as the brief statement she'd given the detective earlier. She hadn't thought of anything extra.

"Let's get something to eat." Suzanne emerged from the small room. "I can't believe Detective Rawson is related to Detective Edgewater. They are so different!"

"I know," Maddie agreed.

Detective Edgewater was in his sixties, and old-fashioned, although he'd become a fan of her coffee and Suzanne's health balls. Detective Rawson, on the other hand, was all business, and seemed to suspect every competitor of killing Margot. But perhaps he had to be like that in the big city. She couldn't imagine him stopping by their coffee truck to say hello and savoring a vanilla cappuccino.

They found a table in the café and scanned the menu. Maddie's stomach growled, reminding her that she hadn't eaten since breakfast, and that had only been one slice of toast – she'd been too nervous about the competition to eat anything heartier.

Suzanne ordered a BLT, and Maddie chose lasagna.

Once the waitress took their order, Suzanne leaned across the table, as if she didn't want anyone else to hear.

"Did the detective tell you Margot was definitely drowned?"

"Yes." Maddie kept her voice low. "He said that so far the preliminary results were that drowning was the cause of death."

"And that it seems unlikely that it was self-inflicted," Suzanne added. "So nobody hit her on the head first – they just drowned her in the mocha vat." She looked thoughtful.

"Yes," Maddie agreed. "Which might mean the murder wasn't planned." She paused.

"But what was she doing in the ballroom alone before round two started?" Suzanne asked.

"Checking the stations were all set up correctly for the next round?"

"Maybe. Or maybe …" Suzanne leaned over the table even further toward Maddie "… she was meeting someone there. Like a friend – someone she was close to – or thought she was. They got into a fight and the other person pushed her into the mocha vat and left her there to drown."

Cold fingers of dread crawled down Maddie's spine.

"Promise me we won't ever get to that stage," she said.

"Of course not," Suzanne said vehemently. "We're BFFs forever. I've got your back and you've got mine – and that's the way it's been ever since we met."

"True." The dread eased as she remembered the first day they'd met in middle school. They'd continued to be best friends through the years and now they had their own coffee truck. And Suzanne seemed ecstatic that Maddie had started dating her brother Luke.

The waitress arrived with their order, and after thanking her, they dug in. Maddie didn't realize how hungry she was until she took her first bite, then couldn't stop until she'd eaten every morsel of the delicious lasagna.

Suzanne seemed just as hungry, not speaking until after she'd popped the last of her BLT into her mouth, crispy bacon garnished with sliced tomato and lettuce with a morsel of white toast.

"There's Connor – and Ellie." Suzanne's eyes widened as she swung her head to the left.

Maddie followed her gaze. Ellie and Connor had just come into the café, and sat at a table.

"Do you think all the people who made it to round two will be eating here tonight?" she asked her friend.

"That would mean Diana, Brad, and the other three finalists." Suzanne counted on her fingers. "I didn't get to meet them – did you?"

"No." Maddie shook her head. "I think their espresso stations were behind mine."

"We should find out more about them."

"Why?" Maddie frowned. "I don't think we're really suspects, do you? We have an alibi for the approximate time of the murder – we were here, in this café."

"We've given Fred Beldon an alibi as well," Suzanne added. "He was here eating a huge plate of something at the same time we were here."

"So we should let the detective do his job," Maddie said.

"But what if he doesn't catch the killer before next weekend, when everyone comes back to compete in round two? You could be in danger." Suzanne looked worried.

"So could you," Maddie pointed out.

They stared at each other.

"Which means we should help investigate," Suzanne stated. She overrode Maddie's objection. "At least until we know for sure we're not suspects."

"We can't get in the detective's way," Maddie warned.

"Of course not." Suzanne waved her hand in the air as if the thought had never occurred to her.

"And we'll be going home tomorrow. Back to Trixie and Brewed from the Bean."

"I know. But if we keep our eyes and ears open, we might stumble across a piece of crucial information that we can take to the detective," Suzanne said.

"As long as that's all we do," Maddie said cautiously. All she wanted to do was go home back to Estherville and practice for round two. As well as spend time with Trixie – and Luke.

"Of course," Suzanne assured her, her features lively.

Perhaps in another life Suzanne would have been a police detective?

Before Maddie could voice that thought, Brad appeared in the entrance, before finding a table.

"That's Brad," Suzanne murmured.

"Yes," Maddie agreed. They watched him speak to a waitress and then peruse a menu.

"I guess this is a convenient place to eat," Maddie remarked, pushing away her plate.

"Do you want dessert?" Suzanne asked, her gaze darting from Connor and Ellie to Brad.

"No, thanks, I'm full."

"All we need now is Diana Swift," Suzanne murmured.

"Maybe she's been cleared and gone home, if she lives in the city," Maddie suggested. "Oh!" A thought struck her.

She looked around, but nobody seemed interested in their conversation, including the other competitors. "Maybe it's my imagination, but when the detective asked Diana if she knew the victim, I thought she hesitated before saying she didn't."

Suzanne's eyebrows lifted. "You mean she might have met her before today?"

"That's right." Maddie nodded.

"Hmm." Suzanne looked thoughtful. "If Diana knew Margot, that might explain why Margot didn't mark her as low as everyone else."

"You're right." Was that why Diana had denied knowing the victim? Had

Margot deliberately given elegant Diana higher scores in round one? Why?

"But Diana already pointed out how unlikely she'd be to kill a judge who gave her a better score than her competitors." Suzanne wrinkled her nose.

"I remember."

"So even if Diana knew Margot previously, why would she kill her?"

"What if it wasn't Diana? What if it was someone from Margot's personal life?" Maddie suggested. "Maybe they did it here because they knew there would be a lot of potential suspects to keep the police busy."

"Good point." Suzanne snapped her fingers.

"But how would the killer know the mocha vat would be there?" Maddie poked holes in her own theory. "There was no weapon used."

"Fred wheeling in the mocha vat seemed to come as a total surprise to Margot." Suzanne picked up the thread. "It doesn't seem as if she knew that was going to happen today."

"So she wouldn't have told someone in her personal life, "Fred Beldon is bringing a huge vat full of his terrible mocha beverage to the competition," which might have given the murderer the idea in the first place."

"Exactly." Suzanne looked glum. "No wonder the detective considers us all suspects."

CHAPTER 4

Maddie and Suzanne left the coffee shop and headed up to their room.

"I think you should do a Coffee Vision spell," Suzanne said as they stepped inside their hotel room.

"Okay." Maddie wouldn't mind a cup of coffee now, even if she couldn't make a proper espresso with the hotel coffee maker.

It didn't seem to matter what kind of coffee she made, whether instant, drip, or using a fancy espresso machine, the spell had worked each time she cast it, since she was seven years old.

Maddie turned on the coffee maker, and waited for the water to heat, then for the coffee to drip into the pot.

When it was ready, she cleared her mind and looked into her cup.

"Show me," she whispered.

The black surface of the coffee swirled, then cleared.

An image of Luke appeared – standing outside her front door. Maddie smiled.

"Well?" Suzanne asked eagerly. "Did you see the murderer confessing?"

"No. But I did see your brother – coming to visit me."

"Since the Coffee Vision spell shows what's possible in the next twenty-four hours, that doesn't surprise me." Suzanne laughed. "I think he's crazy about you."

"Really?" Maddie held her breath.

"Yep." Suzanne nodded. "You two have fun, and make sure I'm the maid of honor."

"Suzanne!" Maddie blushed. "We've only gone out a few times."

"It's a shame Luke had to work today, otherwise …" Suzanne waggled her eyebrows.

"Stop that!" Maddie threw a pillow at her. She couldn't even think about Luke and herself in the same hotel room, even in this kind of situation – at the request of the police.

Suzanne laughed. "Okay, I'll stop teasing. But it would be so cool if we were sisters one day."

"I know." Maddie smiled at her friend.

"Do you think you'll ever tell him about … you know … *Wytchcraft for the Chosen* and the fact that you're a witch?"

"I don't know." Maddie shrugged, her lighthearted mood turning somber. If she and Luke were meant to be together, surely he would understand if she showed him the ancient tome and told him about her limited ability (so far) for spell casting?

But what if he recoiled from her in horror? Suzanne was the only person she'd told and luckily, she hadn't reacted badly. Her friend had been super supportive since day one. But Maddie knew some people viewed witches with suspicion, while others didn't believe in paranormal anything. And she and Luke had spent minimal time together so far. She didn't know what his views were on the supernatural.

"I don't think he scares easily," Suzanne said. "But it's your decision. I'll be there for you no matter what you decide."

"Thanks." Maddie gave her a grateful smile.

"What should we do about the full moon on Monday night?" Suzanne asked. "I can come over to your place and see what happens."

"Okay," Maddie replied. "Maybe there will be a new spell I'll be able to cast."

"That would be so cool." Suzanne grinned. "And I know Trixie will be up for it. She might even show us which spell you should try from the book."

"True," Maddie replied. "She did that last month, remember?"

"Yep." Suzanne nodded.

Maddie yawned. "I think I'll take a nice soak in the tub – unless you want it first?"

"Go ahead." Suzanne flopped down on the bed and turned on the TV remote. "I'll see if there's anything interesting to watch."

Maddie relaxed in a warm bubble bath, the jasmine scented foam lifting her spirits. It was a shame she didn't have pajamas to wear tonight or clean clothes for tomorrow, but right now, the hot water was doing her good.

When she finished and put on her clothes again, she found Suzanne engrossed in a legal drama.

"Your turn," Maddie said, sitting down on the other bed.

A commercial break came on, upbeat music playing.

"Okay." Suzanne got up and headed toward the bathroom. "Let me know what happens with that show."

Maddie allowed herself to get wrapped up in the fictional story of a woman accused of embezzlement. Once Suzanne finished in the bathroom, the end credits were rolling.

"She was innocent," Maddie told her. "And the guy who stole the money was caught."

"Good." Suzanne slid into bed. "I just hope they find today's killer as quickly."

"Me too." Maddie turned off her bedside light, guessing that it probably wouldn't be that easy.

***

The next morning, Maddie and Suzanne ate a quick breakfast in the coffee shop, but to their disappointment, they didn't spot any of the other competitors who had made it through to round two.

Just as they finished their meal, Maddie's cell phone rang. She answered it, Detective Rawson's voice making her wary at first, until he told her the news they were waiting to hear – they could now go home.

"Yay!" Suzanne cheered when Maddie ended the call. "I can't want to get out of these clothes." She plucked at her green t-shirt.

"I know what you mean," Maddie said ruefully. If her Coffee Vision came true, she didn't want Luke to see her in two-day old clothes, even if last night's jasmine scented bubbles had lingered on her skin.

"I bet Trixie will be pleased when we come to collect her."

"So will Mom," Maddie replied. She appreciated her mother looking after Trixie, but she wasn't used to pets.

Two hours later, they arrived at Maddie's parents' house.

"It's good to be back." Suzanne stretched as she got out of the car.

"Yes." Maddie wondered if Trixie would be cross with her for leaving her overnight, despite their telepathic "conversation". It was the first time they'd been apart since the Persian had scampered into her life just over a year ago.

Before Maddie could knock on the door, it swung open, her mother smiling at her.

"Here she is, Trixie," her mother said, looking down at the fluffy white cat.

Trixie rubbed against the older woman's gray slacks, then lifted her head to greet Maddie, a pleased expression on her face.

"Mrrow."

"I'm sure Trixie knew you were arriving – she kept trotting to the front door. And I know you didn't want her going outside in a strange neighborhood."

"Thanks, Mom." Maddie bussed her mother's cheek. "I really appreciate you looking after Trixie for me."

"It was no trouble at all," her mother declared. "Was it, Trixie?"

The cat looked up at Maddie's mother and gave a demure, "Mrrow."

"Hi, Mrs. Goodwell." Suzanne bounced up to the porch. "Hi, Trixie."

"Mrrow." Trixie rubbed herself against Suzanne's jean-clad leg, then looked up at Maddie.

"I missed you," Maddie murmured, crouching down.

Trixie jumped into her arms and snuggled against her, her raspy purr filling Maddie's heart with warmth.

"I'm glad she's not mad at me for not coming home last night," Maddie remarked.

"You'll have to tell me what happened." Maddie's mother gestured for them to come in. "I've got all of Trixie's belongings ready for you, but you girls must want something to drink."

"That would be great, Mrs. Goodwell," Suzanne said.

Once they were seated at the kitchen table that sported a vase of yellow daffodils, Maddie quickly filled in her mother on what happened. Through the kitchen window, she spied her father mowing the lawn and waved to him, the drone of the lawnmower a familiar weekend sound.

"That's wonderful that you made it to the final round, dear." Her mother beamed. Then her face fell. "But it's terrible that you're mixed up in murder – again."

"I know," Maddie replied. Her mother didn't need to tell *her* that.

"I'm sure the police will figure out who did it," Suzanne said, her tone lively.

Maddie risked a glance at her, but Suzanne didn't elaborate.

"I'm sure they will, too," Maddie's mom said. "And you girls should be safe here in Estherville. The killer probably lives in Seattle." She frowned. "I just hope they catch whoever did it before next weekend – I don't want you girls to be in danger for round two."

"I'm sure we won't be," Suzanne reassured her. "There'll probably be police there in case the killer shows up."

"I just hope he – or she – doesn't want to murder someone else." Maddie shuddered. Trixie must have sensed her uneasiness, because she nestled deeper in Maddie's arms.

After they drank their hot chocolate – the day was cool enough to enjoy it – they said goodbye to Maddie's mother. Trixie showed a marked disinclination to hop into her carrier, so Maddie held her securely while they walked out to the car, while Suzanne carried Trixie's belongings.

"Your mom seems really taken with Trixie," Suzanne said as they set off to Suzanne's house.

"I know," Maddie replied, looking at the Persian in the rear-view mirror. "What did you do to her, Trix?"

"Mrrow," Trixie said smugly, looking pleased with herself.

"Maybe she didn't do any actual magic," Suzanne said slowly. "Maybe she just used her natural feline charms to enchant your mother – the same ones any cat has."

"Broomf!" Trixie looked indignant.

"Sorry, Trix," Suzanne replied. "I know your charms are super impressive."

"Mrrow." Trixie seemed mollified.

"I'm just glad Mom's warmed to her," Maddie said. "I might have to ask if she can stay the night next weekend when we

83

go back to Seattle for round two – just in case something else happens."

Trixie looked like she didn't know whether to be happy or sad at the news.

"Like another judge being murdered." Suzanne nodded.

"I hope not." Maddie grimaced.

***

Maddie pulled up outside her house. She and Trixie had dropped off Suzanne, and all Maddie wanted to do was to flop on the couch and relax.

Then she remembered the Coffee Vision spell she'd cast last night. Luke might drop by today!

"Come on, Trixie." She carried the cat to the porch and set her down on the ground while she unlocked the door.

Trixie scampered inside, seemingly glad she was home.

Maddie had a quick shower and changed into clean clothes, before loading the washing machine.

Before the cycle finished, the doorbell rang.

"Hi, Luke," she said breathlessly. He stood in front of her, wearing jeans and a charcoal t-shirt.

"Hi, Maddie." He smiled down at her, warmth in his green eyes. His auburn hair was cut short in a way that suited his attractive features.

"Mrrow!" Trixie came to the door and looked up at him, tilting her head to the side.

"Hi, Trixie." Luke bent down to stroke her.

The Persian practically fluttered her whiskers at him, rubbing her cheek against his hand and allowing him to pet her.

"Come in," Maddie said, holding the door open, stifling a giggle at Trixie's behavior. She was also a little envious of her cat. Right now she was getting more attention from Luke than Maddie was!

Luke followed her into the kitchen, Trixie importantly leading the way.

The Coffee Vision spell had worked! Over the years, Maddie had realized that the spell only showed a possibility of what could happen in the next twenty-four hours – it wasn't absolute. But she was glad that the vision she'd seen last night in the cup of coffee had come true.

"Would you like a latte?" She gestured to the espresso machine in the kitchen.

"Sure." His eyes crinkled at the corners. "But that's not the reason I stopped by. I wanted to say hi."

"Hi," she replied breathlessly.

They stood staring at each other for long seconds, then Maddie busied herself with the machine. Trixie hopped up onto a chair at the table, looking from Maddie to Luke and back again.

The machine hissed and burred as Maddie pulled an espresso shot and steamed the milk, certain her cheeks were burning. Why did Luke have that effect on her?

She handed him the coffee, her fingers brushing his. He sat opposite Trixie at the kitchen table.

"Thanks." He smiled and lifted the latte glass to his lips. After an appreciate sip, he placed it back down on the table and turned all his attention to her.

"How was Seattle?" he asked.

"Unexpected." Maddie took a deep breath and sat down next to Trixie, too keyed up to make herself a coffee. She filled him in on what had happened yesterday, finishing with, "And now I have to go back to Seattle next weekend to compete in round two – the final round."

"Wow," he said softly as he absorbed her news. "How are you and Suzanne?"

"We're okay," she replied, appreciating his thoughtfulness. "You know your sister – she seems to take everything in her stride."

"I'll call her later and make she's all right. But what about you? Do you still feel like competing next weekend?"

His perceptiveness was one of the qualities that attracted her to him.

"Yes and no," she answered. "I was so nervous yesterday at the beginning of round one that at first I didn't know whether to be relieved or disappointed that round two was postponed. As well as feeling awful that Margot was killed, of course," she added hastily. She didn't want to make light of the judge's death – it had been a terrible thing.

"But now … I don't want to chicken out of the final round. I would be disappointed in myself if I did. And Suzanne has been very enthusiastic about this competition."

"I know." He chuckled. "But don't let my sister talk you into something you're not comfortable with."

"I won't." She smiled at him, her heartbeat fluttering. This wasn't the first time since they'd started dating that she'd wondered if Luke "got her". So far, the signs were promising. But what would happen if one day she told him about her witchy abilities?

Don't go there.

It was way too soon to even think about it.

Until now, Trixie had been quiet, seemingly content to let the humans talk. Now, she nudged Maddie's arm, demanding to be petted.

"She's a cutie." Luke smiled at the cat.

"And she knows it." Maddie smiled at Trixie and then across the table at Luke.

Her gaze caught his and held.

"I don't want anything to happen to you, Maddie." He cleared his throat. "I should be able to free up my schedule for next weekend and go to the competition with you and Suzanne."

When she didn't say anything, he added, "If you want me to."

"Mrrow." Trixie answered for her, looking pleased.

"Yes, I'd like that," Maddie replied, sure she was blushing again. She'd only hesitated because she'd been a little overwhelmed at the thought of Luke there, watching her from the audience for the final round. She was flustered just sitting across from him right now! It had been amazing that she'd been able to talk to him coherently on their dates so far – at least she thought she had.

"Great." He smiled.

They chatted for a few more minutes, Luke telling her about his rush order which had been the reason why he hadn't been able to go to Seattle with them yesterday, and how he'd finished it a couple of hours ago.

"I better go." He looked regretful as he pushed back his chair. "I'll call Suzanne and check she's okay." He paused. "Would you like to have dinner

Wednesday night or will you be too busy practicing your mochas for Saturday?"

"I'd love to," she replied quickly.

"Mrrow," Trixie agreed for her.

"I'll pick you up at seven," he told her, as she walked him to the front door, Trixie trotting behind her.

"Okay," she murmured, already wondering what she would wear.

"I'll see you then," he said as he stood on the front porch.

Maddie nodded.

"Unless I stop by Brewed from the Bean before then." He grinned. "I'm sure you're going to win the competition next weekend – your barista skills are amazing."

"Thanks." She told herself to breathe. They were only a couple of inches apart. Was he going to kiss her? He hadn't so far, despite their dates.

She held her breath, but after a nanosecond it seemed that the moment passed.

"Well, I'll see you." He walked slowly down the steps.

"See you," she echoed, watching him head to his car. Why hadn't he kissed her? Would it ever happen?

"Broomf," Trixie grumbled, twining around her legs.

"I know, Trix." Maddie sighed. "Broomf."

CHAPTER 5

Maddie and Suzanne opened up the truck on Monday morning at seven-thirty. Trixie had decided to come too, and sat on her stool inside the truck, "supervising".

"You'll have all week to practice for Saturday," Suzanne remarked as they watched their first customer – a jogger – stagger toward the truck. It was amazing how many joggers didn't carry water with them.

"I thought maybe I could practice for an hour every day," Maddie said, after Suzanne handed the sweating exerciser a bottle of water.

"Unless I persuade all our customers to order a mocha." Suzanne grinned mischievously.

"Suzanne!" Maddie couldn't help laughing.

Her friend quickly sobered. "Luke called me yesterday to check I was okay." She peered at Maddie. "Are you sure you want to go through with the competition? It's okay if you want to drop out."

"What did he say to you?" Maddie frowned.

"Nothing." Suzanne waved a hand in the air. "He was just being a caring big brother. But he did say it was your decision whether to carry on with the competition or not, and that he would support the choice you made." She paused. "And so would I. You're the one competing, not me. He's right. It's your decision."

Warmth flooded Maddie at Luke's thoughtfulness.

"And my decision is to compete next weekend," Maddie stated.

"Yes!" Suzanne's ponytail bounced. "But you know I would have supported you if your answer had been different."

"I know." Maddie touched Suzanne's arm. Before she could say anything more, a shadow loomed over them.

"Good morning, Maddie and Suzanne. And Trixie." Detective Edgewater stood in front of the serving window. In his sixties and portly, he had been the detective in charge of the previous murders in Estherville.

"Hi, Detective Edgewater." Suzanne smiled at him. "Would you like your usual?" Her gaze strayed to the empty plastic domed plate, her expression falling. "We don't have any health balls this morning, unfortunately – it was a busy weekend."

"So I heard," he replied, pulling out his wallet. "I'll just have my usual."

"Coming right up." Maddie busied herself making a vanilla cappuccino for the detective.

"And how are you, Maddie?" he asked, concern in his voice.

"I'm okay." She looked up from the espresso machine and attempted a smile. "It was a shock for both of us finding Margot Wheeler like that."

"I'll bet." He nodded.

"Who told you?" Suzanne demanded, taking his money.

"Detective Rawson, my nephew," he replied. "He also asked me to keep an eye on you two – make sure you don't get into any trouble."

"As if we would!" Suzanne's voice was indignant as she handed him his change.

"Uh-huh." He sounded as if he didn't believe her. "The Seattle police have got this all in hand. I don't want you two getting involved. Are we clear?"

"Yes." Maddie nodded as she handed him his drink. "I'm going to be practicing for round two next weekend, anyway."

"Good." The detective looked pleased. "What about you, Suzanne?"

"I'm going to be helping Maddie," Suzanne declared, her expression indicating that he couldn't possibly find anything wrong with that.

"Uh-huh," he repeated, then took a sip of his cappuccino. Pleasure creased his face as he swallowed. "If they had a vanilla cappuccino contest, I'm sure you'd win, Maddie."

"Thanks, Detective Edgewater." Maddie smiled.

"Just don't get involved this time," he warned. "The police will find out who the murderer is." With that parting advice, he headed across the town square toward the sheriff's station, a couple of blocks away.

"Well," Suzanne fumed. "I don't know why he—"

"He's got a point, Suze. There have already been two murders in Estherville."

"Which we helped solve."

"Yes, but this one happened in Seattle. And we – I – need to stay focused on the competition."

"Exactly." Suzanne's expression lightened. "So if we keep our eyes and ears open as I believe I mentioned on the weekend, we might discover a crucial piece of information that we can give to the police – Detective Edgewater's nephew."

"That wasn't exactly what I meant."

"I know what you meant." Suzanne's mouth quirked up at the corners. "But what if the police can't solve it? What if they don't have the right kind of knowledge?"

"Like what?" Maddie stared at her friend.

"Coffee knowledge," Suzanne said triumphantly.

"Mrrow!"

"See? Trixie agrees with me." Suzanne beamed at the Persian.

Maddie sighed. "Fine. So if we come across some obscure tidbit of coffee knowledge that we don't think the detective in Seattle knows about, we'll call him."

"Or we could go and visit him."

"We'll call him," Maddie said firmly. "It will take us two hours to drive to Seattle, and what if he's out of the office? We'd have to wait for him and meanwhile the truck will be closed which means lost revenue."

"Spoilsport." Suzanne mock-pouted. Then she brightened. "It's the full moon tonight. Maybe something in *Wytchcraft for the Chosen* will point us in the right direction and we'll discover who the murderer is!"

***

That night, Maddie, Trixie and Suzanne sat on the sofa in Maddie's living room, the ancient book *Wytchcraft for the Chosen* on Maddie's lap.

"Mrrow." Trixie gently pawed the cover of the book.

"Do you want me to open it?" Maddie asked.

"Mrrow!"

"I think that means yes." Suzanne grinned.

Maddie carefully opened the centuries old book, fly-spotted paper with flowing handwriting in black ink meeting her gaze. There were all kinds of spells in this book, but until recently she'd only been able to cast one spell – the Coffee Vision spell.

"Mrrow." Trixie urged her to keep turning the pages.

"I wonder if there'll be a new spell in here you haven't seen before," Suzanne mused, her eyes alight with excitement.

There were over one hundred spells in the magical book. Although Maddie had pored over the tome numerous times for the last twenty years, even she couldn't remember exactly every single spell. And Suzanne was right – last month she'd come across a spell she hadn't remembered before – and when she'd tried it, it had worked!

She just hoped she would never have to cast it again.

Trixie's turquoise gaze met her eyes, as if the feline was thinking the same thing.

"Mrrow." Trixie's paw gently patted a page.

"How to enhance your looks," Maddie read out.

"You don't need that spell." Suzanne giggled. "Luke already thinks you're hot."

"Suzanne!" Maddie blushed but she couldn't contain the smile spreading over her face. "Do you really think so?"

"I know so." Suzanne nodded.

Maddie was just about to tell Suzanne about her upcoming date with Luke on Wednesday night, when Trixie snagged her attention.

"Mrrow." Trixie patted the book which Maddie interpreted as "Turn the page".

"The Coffee Vision spell." Suzanne read out. "You already know how to do that one."

"Yep." Maddie turned a few pages, none of the spells grabbing her attention.

"What do you think, Trix?" Maddie asked. "Is there a special spell in here tonight?"

"Mrrow." Trixie seemed to nod, her eyes gleaming.

"I think she said yes," Suzanne said. "Keep turning the pages."

Maddie, Suzanne, and Trixie peered at each page, but Maddie didn't feel the little tug deep inside that urged her to pause at any of them. Finally, with the golden full moon shining down on them through a chink in the drapes, Maddie hesitated. Something felt different about *this* spell.

"How to move an object," she read out slowly.

"Mrrow!" Trixie placed her paw carefully on the ancient page.

"Is this the one?" Suzanne asked, her voice hushed.

"I think so," Maddie murmured, feeling a little tug toward the page.

"Maybe you better write it down," Suzanne whispered.

"Good idea." Maddie reached for a pad and a pen that she'd put on the coffee table. Sometimes it wasn't practical to race home and look up the new spell she needed when she actually required it. The events of last month had taught her that.

She carefully wrote down the spell, Trixie and Suzanne peering over her shoulder.

How to move an object:
Say these words three times:
With a wave of my hand I bid thee here!
Wave your hand in the direction you want the object to move to.

"Do you think you'll need to use it?" Suzanne asked.

"I don't know." Maddie scanned the lines she'd copied down. "But I'll put it in my purse in case I need it."

"Too bad we haven't found a spell that guarantees you winning round two next weekend," Suzanne teased.

"Mrrow!" Trixie agreed.

"You know I would never do something like that," Maddie protested.

"I know." Suzanne nodded. "The whole personal gain thing. But you must admit it's fun to think about it."

"Maybe if you're not a witch."

They finished looking through *Wytchcraft for the Chosen* but no other spells jumped out. When they were done, Suzanne stretched and yawned.

"I think I'll go home. It's late and it's been a busy three days."

"That's for sure." Maddie smiled ruefully.

"Mrrow!"

Maddie and Suzanne looked at each other and laughed.

"She did win over Mom," Maddie said.

"That's right." Suzanne grinned at Trixie. "I'll see you tomorrow, Trix. You, too, Mads."

After Suzanne left, Maddie got ready for bed, wondering if she would ever have the need to cast the How to Move an Object spell and if it would work.

***

The next day, Trixie pawed Maddie awake, patting her arm gently.

"I'm up," Maddie groaned, blinking sleep out of her eyes.

"Mrrow." Trixie peered at her, then gave her a soft nose kiss, her whiskers skimming Maddie's cheeks.

"Thanks, Trixie." The gesture touched Maddie's heart, and she wondered how she'd managed to live without a pet until Trixie came into her life.

After she fed Trixie, showered, and ate granola, she and Trixie headed to the town square in the truck.

A few minutes later, Suzanne arrived, and soon they were serving their first customers.

Maddie realized with a guilty start that yesterday she hadn't practiced for the competition. Oops. Better not tell Suzanne!

After the early morning rush, where Maddie made eight mochas (which surely counted as practice) she and Suzanne flopped down on their stools, sitting on either side of Trixie.

"Phew." Suzanne gulped down bottled water.

"I know," Maddie agreed, sipping the mocha she'd made herself – which was more practice (or so she told herself).

"Mixed up in murder again, Maddie?" A whining nasal voice assaulted her ears. A stout forty-something woman with cropped, jet black hair approached the serving window. Claudine Claxton – Maddie's nemesis and former boss.

"What are you talking about?" Suzanne jumped to her feet and frowned.

"I heard what happened in Seattle." Claudine wagged her finger. "You've got to be more careful, Maddie."

Trixie screwed up her face and looked like she wanted to growl at the interloper, but was trying to refrain.

"What happened has nothing to do with me." Maddie rose from the stool.

"Are you sure?" Claudine taunted.

"Yes, we're sure." Suzanne said as she and Maddie moved together to the serving window to stare down the older woman.

"First the coffee festival, and now this." Claudine tsked. "And don't forget one of your customers died as well a while ago."

How could Maddie forget? She'd seen her customer's death in a Coffee Vision spell and hadn't been able to save her.

"And your point is?" Suzanne glared at Claudine.

"Maybe you killed the judge to give yourself an edge."

"What?" Maddie stared at her nemesis.

"She gave you low marks so you killed her," Claudine said smugly.

"Where did you get this information?" Suzanne demanded.

"Oh, you know." Claudine shrugged. "Here and there."

"For your information, Maddie – and I – were allowed to return home," Suzanne told her. "If Maddie was a suspect, don't you think she'd still be in Seattle?"

"That's because the detective is stupid," Claudine remarked. "I would have locked you up. But," she considered, "if you make a run for it now, everyone will know. You can't hide in a small town, Maddie Goodwell."

"I'm not hiding." Maddie found her voice. "Brewed from the Bean is open for business as usual. And I'm sure the police will catch the killer."

"Yeah." Suzanne snapped her fingers. "In time for round two next weekend." When Claudine didn't say anything, she continued, "Haven't you heard that Maddie made it to the finals? So why would she kill the judge?"

"So she can win the competition," Claudine finally said, as if she hadn't realized that Maddie had been successful in the preliminary round. "Yeah, that's why Maddie killed her. She was scared she'd get low marks again in the final round and wouldn't win. And we all know that the prize was an entry into the national barista championship."

An expression of envy crossed Claudine's face. Maddie wondered if that was why the older woman was being so poisonous. Did she begrudge Maddie her barista skills?

A lot of townsfolk avoided Claudine's café because of the cheap, terrible coffee that somehow Claudine thought tasted wonderful. But still, she had some customers – Maddie saw them when she walked past the shop.

"Maddie doesn't need to win the competition for everyone to know how incredible her coffee is." Suzanne waved her hand in the air. "She beat out a lot of people on Saturday – that's how good she is. And for your information, that judge marked everyone low. She didn't single out Maddie."

"Suzanne's right," Maddie said, squaring her shoulders. "And since you

weren't there on Saturday, I don't see
how this is any of your business,
Claudine. It's a police matter. And I'm
not going to say another word about it."

"Yeah!" Suzanne folded her arms
across her chest.

"Brrr," Trixie growled, as if in
agreement.

"Fine." Claudine flounced off. "But
you better hope another murder doesn't
take place at the competition next
Saturday, because if there is, I'll point the
police in your direction!"

"Charming." Suzanne shook her head
when Claudine was out of earshot.

"I know."

"Broomf!" Trixie stared after Claudine
until the woman was out of sight, then
shook herself. She turned around a couple
of times on her stool and busied herself
with grooming, looking like a ballerina
with her leg pointed in the air as she
licked her fur into place.

"That woman drives me insane."
Suzanne looked like she was going to get
mad all over again.

"At least you didn't have to work for
her," Maddie said ruefully. When

Claudine had taken over the coffee shop, Maddie had worked for her as long as she could stand it – then she quit, setting up Brewed from the Bean with Suzanne and Trixie. She'd never been happier.

"Let's talk about something else."

"Good idea." Maddie sat on a stool, noticing the tension in her friend's stance. "I know, why don't you get a massage with Ramon? That will help make you feel better."

Suzanne blushed. "I would, but I don't want to leave you and Trixie alone. Not after … *her*. And besides, if anyone needs a massage right now, it should be you."

Suzanne had been urging her to try a massage with Ramon, the town's sexy Spanish masseuse, for a while now, but Maddie had resisted the idea.

Besides, there seemed to be an attraction between Suzanne and Ramon, and Maddie didn't want to get in the middle of it. So far, nothing had happened between them, Suzanne stating that he was a totally professional masseuse. But that didn't stop her from blushing whenever his name was mentioned or when he stopped by the truck for an espresso.

As if on cue, Ramon suddenly appeared at the serving window. In his early forties, he had charcoal hair, liquid brown eyes, olive skin, and an incredibly handsome face.

"Hello, Maddie. And Suzanne. And Trixie." His faint Spanish accent made everything he said sound enticing.

Trixie paused in her grooming to give him a coquettish look.

"Hi Ramon." Suzanne blushed.

"Hi," Maddie greeted him.

"How did you fare in the competition on the weekend?" Ramon asked, his eyes gleaming with interest.

"She made it through to round two – the final round," Suzanne jumped in.

"Excellent." Ramon looked pleased for Maddie.

"Thanks." Maddie smiled at him, appreciating his good looks. But now she was dating Luke, that was all it was – appreciation. Only Luke had the power to touch her heart.

But as she cast a sideways glance at Suzanne, looking happy yet a little flustered, she wondered if Ramon was already touching Suzanne's heart, despite the age gap.

"But I thought the whole competition would only take one day," he continued, his brow puzzled.

"That's because—" Maddie started reluctantly.

"One of the judges was murdered!" Suzanne told him, lowering her voice.

Ramon seemed shocked as Suzanne filled him in on the details.

"I'm glad you two are okay," he said. "And I hope the police catch the killer."

"So do we," Maddie said in a heartfelt voice.

"Don't worry, Ramon, we'll be careful." Suzanne smiled at him.

"I hope so, Suzanne." His brow furrowed. "Murder is a serious business. I do not want you to get hurt."

Suzanne's face softened as she looked at the sexy Spaniard.

"Maddie and I will be together the whole time next Saturday – even when she's competing and I'm sitting in the audience, we'll be in the same room."

"That is good to hear." He nodded. "Good luck for Saturday, Maddie. I hope you win."

"Thanks, Ramon." Maddie touched the espresso machine. "Would you like your usual?"

"Please, Maddie." He dug out his wallet from the pocket of his tailored khaki chinos.

As the machine burred and hissed, she noticed Suzanne and Ramon engaged in what appeared to be lighthearted conversation.

After she handed him his espresso, they waved goodbye to him, watching him stride across the square to his small salon.

"He is just so ... so ..." Suzanne fanned herself.

"I know," Maddie agreed.

Several customers arrived, and after Maddie and Suzanne served them, they both sat down on their stools, grateful for the reprieve.

Then Maddie's heart fluttered as Luke walked up to the serving window.

"Hi, Luke," she breathed.

"Mrrow." Trixie sat up, looking interested.

"What are you doing here?" Suzanne demanded.

"Aren't I allowed to enjoy the best coffee in town?" There was a teasing light in his eyes as he looked at his sister.

"In that case, that will be $4.40 for a large mocha." Suzanne held her hand out. "Maddie needs to practice."

"Suzanne! Luke can have one on the house." Maddie nudged her friend.

"It's okay, Maddie." Luke's eyes crinkled at the corners as he gave his sister the money.

Maddie set to work making his drink, hoping he wouldn't notice how flustered she was.

"How are you, Trixie?"

"Mrrow." Trixie preened at Luke, blinking girlishly at him.

"She definitely likes you," Suzanne observed as she handed him his change.

"No health balls?" He looked disappointed for a second.

"Come by this afternoon," Suzanne told him.

"Here you go." Maddie set the cardboard cup in front of him, an exciting shiver racing up her spine as his fingers grazed hers.

"Thanks." He smiled at her, and she was lost.

"Ahem." Suzanne cleared her throat.

"Oh – yeah." Luke picked up his mocha. "I'll see you tomorrow night, Maddie."

She nodded, watching him walk across the green lawn to the other side of the square.

"What's on tomorrow night?" Suzanne peered at her.

"We're having dinner." Maddie smiled.

"And you didn't tell me?" Suzanne mock-pouted.

"I was going to but then the full moon happened and—"

"I get it." Suzanne said understandingly, then grinned. "You can tell me all about it on Thursday."

Maddie nodded, knowing there might be some details she'd want to keep to herself, like the way she felt when Luke's hand brushed hers. But she'd certainly tell Suzanne as much as she could.

"I've got to make some health balls." Suzanne looked guiltily at the empty platter on the counter. "I could have sold Luke two."

"I can hold the fort if you want to buy the ingredients now." Maddie nodded towards the small grocery store on the other side of the square.

"Good idea." Suzanne cheered up and got out her phone to type out a shopping list. "Last week I came up with a new idea, but with the competition and … everything else, I forgot to tell you." She paused. "Cacao Orange health balls."

"That sounds interesting."

"Wait 'til you try them." Suzanne grinned. "We can be the guinea pigs – and it's my own recipe."

"Go for it," Maddie encouraged.

"I'll see you in a bit. You too, Trixie."

"Mrrow."

Luckily it wasn't too busy while Suzanne was gone. Maddie handled the orders and took the money while Trixie meowed a greeting at her favorite customers.

When Suzanne returned, she was raring to make the health balls.

"If I make them now, they'll be ready in a couple of hours."

Maddie and Trixie watched her process the ingredients, roll them into small balls, then place the cookie tray into the small refrigerator in the truck.

"We can have them for dessert." Suzanne grinned.

Two hours later, when the last of the lunchtime customers had departed, Maddie and Suzanne were ready to try the Cacao Orange balls.

Suzanne popped a ball into her mouth and chewed. Pleasure creased her face.

"Even better than I hoped!"

Trixie watched with wide eyes as Maddie took a tentative bite of hers.

"You're right." She turned to Trixie. "They really are good, Trix – but it would make you sick if you had one."

"Broomf." Trixie looked disappointed.

"Sorry, Trix." Suzanne looked apologetic.

"I can definitely taste the orange zest," Maddie said.

"I know!" Suzanne set the remaining balls on the platter and put a plastic dome over them. "Now all we have to do is sell them ASAP."

And they did. By the time they closed the truck at four o'clock, only two balls were left. Luke had stopped by again, Suzanne making him pay for two, while Maddie blushed in his presence.

"We might as well finish them off." Suzanne offered a Cacao Orange to Maddie, popping the last one in her mouth.

After savoring the treat, Maddie jumped into the driver's seat. She was supposed to practice making mochas when she got home, but right now, all she wanted to do was look forward to her date tomorrow night with Luke.

CHAPTER 6

After Maddie arrived home, she practiced making mochas for an hour in the truck parked in her driveway, made dinner for herself and Trixie, and spent the evening alternatively reading a chick-lit novel and daydreaming about Luke.

When she finally went to bed, Trixie at her side, she knew she would probably dream about Luke that night, too.

The next morning, she and Trixie parked the truck in the town square, Suzanne already waiting for them, her face downcast.

"What's wrong?" Maddie asked as she got out of the truck.

"Have you realized that we haven't spoken to any suspects yet?"

"No." Maddie frowned.

"Mrrow." Trixie seemed to agree with Maddie.

"We have been busy, though," Maddie pointed out.

"I know." Suzanne nodded. "But it's Wednesday already and we have to go back to Seattle on Saturday. What if the killer attends the final round of the competition?"

"I thought we were going to let the Seattle police do their job," Maddie replied as she and Trixie hopped into the back of the truck. The Persian settled on her stool, while Maddie started getting everything ready.

"And we were going to keep our eyes and ears open, remember?" Suzanne scrutinized the espresso machine over Maddie's shoulder. She snapped her fingers, the sound close to Maddie's ear. "I know! You could do a Coffee Vision spell – maybe that will tell us what we should do today."

"Before or after serving our customers?" Maddie asked drily.

"In between." Suzanne waved a hand in the air. "We managed to run the truck and talk to suspects last month, didn't we?"

"Yes." And they'd had to close the truck while doing so.

"So why don't we do that again?" Suzanne looked excited. "But first, cast the Coffee Vision spell."

"You're bossy this morning," Maddie muttered, looking out through the serving hatch. No customers in sight. "Okay," she acquiesced when Suzanne continued to look at her in expectation.

Maddie pulled an espresso shot, deciding she might as well make a mocha for extra practice. When she'd finished, she peered into the microfoam. She focused her mind, the presence of Suzanne and Trixie receding to the background.

"Show me," she whispered.

The foam swirled, then cleared. An image of Diana Swift appeared in the cup.

"Well?" Suzanne asked impatiently.

"All I see is Diana Swift."

"Ooh. Maybe that means we should go visit her and ask her some questions."

"I don't think driving all the way to Seattle today is a good idea." Maddie put her foot down. Sometimes Suzanne's enthusiasms had a tendency to run away with her.

Before Suzanne could answer, a twenty-something guy dressed in a smart business suit ordered a large hazelnut latte.

After that, they barely had a chance to speak until the morning rush was over.

Trixie snoozed through most of it, only seeming to wake up when one of her favorite customers appeared at the window. How did she do it? Maddie wondered. It was like she had some inbuilt telepathy.

But was it really surprising? If the cat was Maddie's familiar, why wouldn't Trixie have some powers of her own? After all, she and Trixie had seemed to communicate telepathically last Saturday.

Maddie made herself a cappuccino and sat down on a stool. She'd offered to make Suzanne one as well, but her friend took a large gulp of bottled water instead.

"I still think we should go and visit Diana," Suzanne continued to argue now that there was a temporary lull.

"I don't think "keeping our eyes and ears open" includes driving one hundred miles to Seattle to ask a suspect questions," Maddie pointed out.

"Semantics," Suzanne said airily. "You agree with me, don't you, Trixie?"

Trixie stared at Suzanne for a moment, then closed her eyes and settled down for another snooze.

Maddie stifled a giggle.

"It looks like I'll have to try another way to convince you," Suzanne continued. Her face brightened. "We can have lunch in Seattle – my treat."

For a second Maddie was tempted. It would be fun to go out and have lunch in the city, instead of eating their sandwiches in the coffee truck as usual. But before she could formulate an answer, a smartly dressed woman stepped up to the window.

Diana Swift.

Maddie's eyes widened. The coffee vision had come true already!

"Hi, Diana." Suzanne stepped to the window with a big smile on her face, somehow managing to hide the fact they'd just been talking about her.

"Hi, Diana," Maddie greeted the posh woman in a more subdued tone.

"Hello, Maddie and Suzanne." Diana smiled. "Oh, is that a Persian?" She gazed at Trixie snoozing on the stool.

As if she heard her name being mentioned, Trixie slowly opened her eyes and blinked.

"Mrrow?" she said questioningly.

"This is Trixie," Maddie said.

"What a sweet little thing," Diana complimented. "She is just darling."

"Thanks." Maddie relaxed. When the health inspector had visited them when they'd first opened for business, Trixie's presence had seemed to go unnoticed by the worker. Maddie had always wondered if Trixie had something to do with that, in a magical way. And her customers didn't seem to think there was anything wrong with Trixie being in the truck.

"What can we do for you, Diana?" Suzanne asked, her expression curious.

Diana laughed. "I would love to try your coffee, Maddie."

"Of course." Maddie smiled. She gestured to the small menu board in front of the counter. "What would you like?"

"How about a regular latte?"

"Coming right up." Maddie busied herself at the machine, determined that the elegant woman wouldn't be disappointed.

"It was such a shock about Margot Wheeler, wasn't it?" Diana mused as Maddie steamed the milk.

"Definitely." Suzanne nodded.

It was on the tip of Maddie's tongue to ask her fellow competitor if she had known the judge previously, but she didn't want to distract herself while making the latte. And, she had to admit, she was a little hesitant in asking such a question.

"Here you go." Maddie placed the cardboard cup on the counter. "On the house." She cast a sideways glance at Suzanne, who nodded discreetly.

"Oh, no, I couldn't." Diana fished in her fawn designer purse for a matching wallet, handing them the correct money.

Suzanne reluctantly took the cash and put it in the register.

Maddie waited while Diana took her first sip.

A smile crossed her face as she tasted and swallowed. After a few more sips, she finally spoke.

"That is wonderful, Maddie." She nodded. "I made the right decision coming here today.

Maddie and Suzanne exchanged a look of curiosity.

"As you know, I'm opening a chain of coffee shops, and the flagship store will be in Seattle. I would like you to be my head barista, Maddie."

Maddie's mouth parted, but she couldn't speak.

"What?" Suzanne squeaked.

"You're ahead of me in the competition so far," Diana said, as if she didn't quite like that fact. "And I need top level baristas to work in my cafes, so I can make my mark in the Seattle coffee scene. I think you're wasted here." Diana cast a look around the empty town square. "Where are your customers?"

"We had our usual morning crowd today," Suzanne spoke up.

"That's right." Maddie nodded. "We both make a living from doing this."

"But I can offer you something more." Diana took another sip of her latte and closed her eyes for a moment, as if savoring the taste. "I'll pay you forty-five thousand dollars per year, plus benefits."

"How much?" Suzanne asked in a choked whisper.

Maddie blinked. She turned to look at Trixie, who also looked surprised at the offer.

"What do you think?" Diana asked when Maddie didn't say anything.

"I think it's very generous of you," Maddie replied slowly, her thoughts in a whirl.

"You'll be earning your salary," Diana told her. "I'd expect you to train the other baristas so they'd be just as good as you – if you or any of them had a sick day, the others would be able to pick up the slack seamlessly – and my customers would know that it didn't matter who made their coffee – it would be a wonderful sensory experience every time."

She continued, "You'd also be responsible for choosing and roasting the beans and trying out new combinations – oh, and coming up with fancy ideas for our monthly speciality drink."

"That sounds amazing," Suzanne admitted.

"It will be." Diana nodded.

Maddie gripped the counter. Some of what Diana offered seemed like a dream come true, apart from training the other baristas to pull an espresso shot just like she did. She didn't know if she would be able to instruct anyone to make it exactly *like she did* – it was something more than learning the technique – she always thought it was an innate ability as well.

Suzanne could make a decent coffee, but she'd always told Maddie that no matter how much she practiced, she would never be able to make espressos as well as Maddie.

And the thought of interchangeable baristas – an image of a line of robots flashed through her mind.

"I'd have to commute to Seattle," Maddie said.

"I'm afraid so," Diana replied. "Unless you decide to move to the city."

Maddie didn't know if she wanted to move to Seattle, even for a great job opportunity. She knew driving two hours in the morning and again in the afternoon would eventually stress her out. And she wouldn't be able to bring Trixie to work, she was sure of that. How could she leave Trixie alone all day long?

And what about Suzanne? They ran Brewed from the Bean as partners. How could she leave her best friend in the lurch?

As if discerning her thoughts, Trixie looked at her with an enquiring expression on her furry face.

She glanced at Suzanne, who was chewing a fingernail, as if waiting for Maddie's decision.

"Thanks, Diana," Maddie finally replied, "but I'm happy here, with Suzanne and Trixie."

"Are you sure?" Diana's brow crinkled, as if she wasn't used to hearing the word no.

"Yes, I'm sure." Maddie smiled.

Suzanne threw her arms around Maddie. "Phew!" Then she drew back as if she realized what she'd just said, an "Oops" look on her face. "But it's totally okay if you want to go for it, Mads," she said sincerely. "I'll understand. Seattle deserves to drink your coffee."

"Maybe one day we can do that – together," Maddie replied, returning her friend's hug, and appreciating her support.

"Together – I love that." Suzanne beamed at her.

Diana cleared her throat.

"Let me know if you change your mind, Maddie." She pulled out a white and silver business card from her purse and handed it to her.

Maddie nodded, glancing down at the impressive-looking card. Perhaps she and Suzanne should get some business cards made after all, if they were going to expand one day.

"What about Ellie?" Maddie asked, trying to think how she could help Diana in her search for a barista. "She's coming first in the competition."

"Yes, I might ask her," Diana replied. "As well as Connor. But you were my first choice, Maddie. You seem very down to earth and reliable."

Maddie wondered if that translated to wearing ordinary clothes (no fairy earrings like Ellie) and not sporting any visible tattoos.

"You know, Maddie, if you really want to make a career for yourself, then you need to network. I belong to a wonderful women's business club in Seattle, and new memberships will be opening soon. I would be happy to propose your name to the group – whether you take up my job offer or not."

"Thank you," Maddie replied, a little surprised at the offer. She and Suzanne had dreams of owning more than one coffee truck, but she didn't think she was a go-getter businesswoman like Diana – or the unfortunate Margot.

Before she could formulate her question, Suzanne jumped in, as if knowing exactly what Maddie was about to ask.

"Was Margot part of this business club?" she asked.

"Why … yes," Diana admitted.

"So you knew her before the competition last weekend," Suzanne persisted.

Diana flushed under her discreet makeup. "Not really," she finally said. "We weren't best friends or anything like that. We saw each other socially on occasion, and of course in club meetings, but other than that I really didn't know her."

"But you told the detective in Seattle that you didn't know her at all," Maddie pointed out gently.

"That was a mistake," Diana admitted, fidgeting with the strap of her purse. "I should have told the police the truth. But I've never come across a dead body before – and I didn't know what to do for the best, apart from getting help. And I didn't want the police to think I was a suspect."

"That's understandable," Maddie sympathized, her mind flashing back to the time when one of their customers was murdered.

"But I really think you should tell the detective about your previous relationship with Margot," Suzanne put in.

"Was that why Margot marked you higher than everyone else?" Maddie asked curiously.

"I think so." Diana Swift flushed a deeper shade of scarlet. "She didn't say anything to me about it, and I didn't even realize she was one of the judges until that morning, when she walked into the ballroom."

"That must be some business club," Suzanne murmured.

"This is why it's important to make contacts, Maddie," Diana stated.

"So you can get an unfair advantage over other competitors?" Suzanne said wryly.

Diana shrugged. "If Margot had proposed that she give me higher marks I would have refused, of course. But," she paused, as if marshaling her thoughts, "I thought it bad form to go up to her after the round one scores were posted and ask her why she gave me better marks than anyone else. Perhaps she preferred my coffee to the other competitors. Perhaps she did judge me with a little favorable bias. But that sort of thing happens in the business world all the time. You either find a way to work with it, or you don't."

Maddie thought she and Suzanne would rather work without that kind of favoritism.

Diana took another sip of her latte, then checked her elegant silver watch studded with diamonds.

"I'm afraid I must go now, girls. Let me know if you change your mind about the job offer, Maddie."

"I will," Maddie promised, knowing deep down she'd made the right decision in refusing the opportunity.

"Wow," Suzanne breathed once Diana had walked across the town square and got into a silver Lexus.

"I know," Maddie agreed.

"Mrrow!"

"At least now we know why Margot marked her higher than you in round one."

"I wonder if she'll tell Detective Rawson?" Maddie mused.

"If she doesn't, we will on Saturday!" Suzanne's expression was fierce, as if she thought Diana had deliberately cheated in the competition.

"Okay," Maddie agreed. "I know we want to expand the business one day, but I don't think I want to belong to that sort of business club."

"Me either." Suzanne's ponytail bounced vigorously as she nodded.

"Mrrow." Trixie looked like she totally agreed with them.

Suzanne sighed. "If Diana was telling the truth, then it seems she didn't have a motive to kill Margot. Why would she?

She was getting an unfair advantage. She might have even won the final round if Margot kept giving her higher marks than the other competitors."

"True," Maddie said thoughtfully, then grimaced. "If I'd known she was going to talk about the murder and her relationship with Margot, I could have cast the Tell the Truth spell."

"Why didn't I think of that?" Suzanne's eyes widened. "It would have been perfect!"

"Apart from the fact I can only use it once per full moon cycle," Maddie reminded her.

"Oh, yeah."

"Mrrow," Trixie agreed.

"Have you got the spell with you?" Suzanne asked.

"No." Maddie shook her head. Last month, she'd copied the spell on a piece of paper, and it had come in handy when she'd been accused of killing the judge at the local coffee festival. But she hadn't even thought she might need it today – she'd been so focused on her date tonight with Luke.

"But as soon as I get home I'll put it in my purse and keep it there."

"Good idea." Suzanne smiled.

The rest of the day passed slowly and quickly at the same time. For once, Maddie clock-watched for the rest of the day, mentally going through her closet. What would she wear tonight?

Once, Suzanne had to wave her hand in front of Maddie's face to get her attention.

"I think we should visit some of the suspects tomorrow," Suzanne suggested.

"What?" Maddie said absently, checking the time on her watch yet again. One minute to four. Close enough. She started shutting down the espresso machine. "Okay."

"Great! We can leave here as soon as we've handled the early morning crowd."

Maddie stared at Suzanne's beaming face, wondering what she had just agreed to. Whatever it was, it made her best friend seem very happy, and surely that couldn't be a bad thing – could it?

CHAPTER 7

Maddie drove herself to work Thursday morning, wrapped in a fluffy pink cloud. She'd had the best time with Luke last night. They'd dined at a new bistro in town, and then afterward they'd walked through the brightly lit town square, before sitting in his car and just talking for a while.

Afterward, he'd driven her home, spending a few minutes petting Trixie who seemed to enjoy the attention, before promising to come and see her compete in round two on Saturday.

He hadn't kissed her – yet. But that was okay, Maddie told herself. She'd been crushing on Luke for years, and now that her dream had come true and she was actually dating him, she didn't want anything to ruin it, including moving too quickly.

But, she wondered, was there such a thing as moving too slowly? Or – did Luke feel the same way she did and didn't want to rush things either?

Hi!" Suzanne greeted her as she got out of the driver's side of the truck, then peered inside. "No Trixie?"

"I thought I should leave her at home today," Maddie replied, "since it sounded like we were doing something later this morning."

"That's right." Suzanne grinned. "I thought we could go and visit Ellie."

Maddie stared at her friend. "We're going to Seattle?"

"Don't tell me you weren't tempted by my offer yesterday," Suzanne teased. Then she sobered. "It's Thursday already, Mads. If we don't try to do something, the killer could be running around the competition on Saturday, maybe looking for his next victim!"

"I know." Maddie sighed.

"And while we're talking to Ellie, we can try out her coffee," Suzanne tempted.

"I would love to try her mocha," Maddie admitted. "Or would that be sort of cheating, since we have to make mochas in the competition on Saturday?"

"Of course it's not!"

"Maybe I'll try her latte instead," Maddie mused. "After all, she's coming first in the competition after the latte round last Saturday."

"Okay." Suzanne began helping Maddie set up the truck for their first customers. "And I'll try her mocha." She grinned mischievously.

Maddie shook her head in mock-disapproval as she opened the serving window.

"How was your date with my brother?" Suzanne asked.

"Good," Maddie replied, a dreamy smile on her face.

"Come on, you have to give me more than that."

Maddie gave her the brief highlights – what they ate for dinner – pork medallions with a honey glaze for her and a rib eye steak for Luke – the stroll in the town square, and then going home. She wanted to keep part of her date to herself so she didn't tell Suzanne about sitting in Luke's car and just talking for a while.

She finished with, "And he's coming to watch me compete on Saturday."

"Awesome!" Suzanne high-fived her. "He can ride with us."

Maddie wasn't sure if that was going to make her even more nervous before the final round – spending two hours in an enclosed space with Luke – despite Suzanne chaperoning.

The first wave of customers approached the truck. This morning, there hadn't been any thirsty joggers, but caffeine deprived employees made up for them. By the time the lull arrived, it was nearly ten o'clock.

"Perfect timing." Suzanne closed the cash register with a little *bang*. "We can leave for Seattle now, visit Ellie and sample her coffee, then have lunch somewhere." She held up her phone. "I was checking online reviews last night and I've found an "authentic"—" she air-quoted the word "–burger bar with grass-fed beef and all the trimmings."

Maddie brightened. It would be fun to have lunch with Suzanne without the pressure of serving customers.

"My treat," Suzanne added persuasively.

"Done." This time, Maddie high-fived Suzanne.

"I hope Trixie doesn't mind she's going to miss out," Suzanne said.

Maddie pressed a couple of buttons on her phone and showed Suzanne the screen. "I don't think so."

The live camera feed showed Trixie lying on the sofa, her furry white stomach offered up to the sun streaming in through the window, seemingly fast asleep. *Wytchcraft for the Chosen* lay next to her.

"So cute!"

They locked up the truck, Maddie leaving a sign in the window that stated they would be closed for the next few hours.

"Or maybe I should say closed until tomorrow." Maddie made a face as she calculated the driving distance to the city. Two hours there, two hours to come home, plus talking to Ellie, and having lunch at the burger place. Probably around six hours, total. At that rate they'd be lucky to get back here for four o'clock, their usual closing time.

"I know," Suzanne agreed. "But we've got to do *something*, Mads."

"Like leaving it to the police?" Maddie suggested wryly.

"Pooh!" Suzanne waved a hand in the air. "I thought we agreed that our – your – coffee knowledge could help crack the case. And all we're doing is trying Ellie's coffee and having lunch somewhere fun."

"Okay," Maddie gave in as she usually did with Suzanne. "But only today, agreed? We can't keep closing the truck for hours – or even a whole day. We're already going to be closed again on Saturday."

"I know." Suzanne sobered. "But I think it's worth it if we can help the police solve the murder. Don't you?"

Maddie nodded, knowing her friend was right, even if she tended to get a little overenthusiastic at times.

Suzanne brandished a car key. "We can take my car today. I even drove here this morning instead of walking, so we wouldn't waste any time."

They jumped into Suzanne's sporty little red car. She'd bought it used a while ago, and Luke had fixed it up for her. But since she lived only a couple of blocks from the town square, she usually walked to work.

They listened to 1980s Brit Pop on the way to Seattle, the local radio station having a retro pop music day. The upbeat, infectious rhythms brightened Maddie's mood, and by the time Suzanne threaded her way to a café near the hotel where the competition had been held last Saturday, she was glad she'd agreed to Suzanne's plan.

Suzanne found a parking space right next to the café.

"I don't want to know how: one, you know where Ellie works, and two, how you snagged that spot," Maddie teased. Not for the first time, she wondered if Suzanne had some latent witchy abilities that she wasn't aware of.

"It was pretty easy to discover where she worked," Suzanne said airily. "She told Connor, remember? Plus I looked up the competitors on the website and it had their occupations, and this café was listed," she admitted. "The parking spot was just luck."

Maddie followed her friend into the small café. It had a hipster, serious coffee vibe enhanced by the scent of roasted beans and chocolate.

"Mmm." Maddie closed her eyes in appreciation.

"If the coffee tastes half as good as the smell, I'm going to have a *delicious* mocha." Suzanne looked guilty for a second. "Although I'm sure yours are better," she added loyally.

"It's okay." Maddie touched her friend's arm. "She's coming first in the competition for a reason."

They walked over to the counter and ordered. Maddie's stomach started rumbling, but she was looking forward to sampling the "authentic" burgers at lunch that Suzanne had told her about. The latte should hold her until then.

Only half the tables were taken, but there were several office workers standing in the pick-up area, waiting for their to-go orders.

"I asked the server if Ellie was working today and she is," Suzanne murmured as they threaded their way to a vacant table, world music playing softly from the speakers high up on the walls.

"She's going to come and see us in a few minutes when she has a break."

"What are we going to say to her?" Maddie asked.

"We could ask her if Diana has approached her with a job offer," Suzanne suggested. "And we can talk about coffee – well, you and Ellie can talk about coffee and I can tell her how delicious her mocha is – even if it isn't."

"Suzanne!" Maddie shook her head in jest.

A server at the pick-up counter called out their names. Maddie went to get them, Suzanne staying at the table in order to "save" it. When Maddie arrived at the counter she looked for Ellie in the back but couldn't see her. Standing on tip-toes, she finally glimpsed a flash of blonde hair on the left.

Steam rose from the drinks as she carried them back to the table.

"Let's see how good she is." Suzanne cupped her hands around her mug.

Maddie stared down at the fancy glass holding her regular latte. Ellie's barista skills had her coming in first place so far, making this very drink. What did it taste like?

She took a small sip, appreciating the foam, noting how the latte hadn't split. High quality coffee beans, different to the ones she used, plus the skill of the barista, made it an excellent latte.

"Delish." Suzanne settled back in the chrome chair. "This mocha is awesome."

"So is this latte."

"But I like yours better," Suzanne added loyally.

Maddie smiled at her friend's thoughtfulness, took another sip, then an idea hit her. She unzipped her purse, and checked inside.

"Do you think I should use the Tell the Truth spell on Ellie?" she whispered to Suzanne.

"Yes!" Suzanne's eyes lit up. "Good idea. Otherwise, we might waste the opportunity of asking her questions."

Maddie nodded, glancing at the piece of paper in her hand containing the spell.

The next second, Ellie walked over to their table.

"Janine said you wanted to see me?" she asked.

The oversized apron she wore emphasized her slight build. Apart from the fact Ellie wasn't wearing fairy earrings, she looked just as she had on Saturday. Maddie decided that even without the earrings she still looked ethereal.

"We met last Saturday at the barista competition," Suzanne began. "I'm Suzanne and this is Maddie. She's coming third."

"Oh yes," Recognition crossed her face. "What can I do for you?"

"We couldn't resist a chance to try your coffee," Suzanne continued. "And this mocha is great!"

"I love your latte," Maddie added. "Especially the beans you used."

"They're single origin beans from Ethiopia," Ellie informed her. "I roast them myself."

Maddie nodded, thinking if anyone deserved to win the competition it was Ellie.

Should she cast the Tell the Truth spell now? She fingered the piece of paper in her hand, hoping it wouldn't crackle and draw unwanted attention.

Before she could make up her mind, they were accosted by a loud male voice.

"There you are, Ellie." A blustery man in his sixties approached them. It was Fred Beldon, the mocha sponsor from the competition.

"Oh, hi." Ellie's cheeks flushed.

"Is your boss in?" the man asked, then seemed to notice Maddie and Suzanne. "Hi, I'm Fred Beldon."

"We know," Suzanne said. "We were at the barista competition last weekend. Maddie is one of the finalists."

Fred nodded. "That's great. Do you two gals run a coffee shop? I can give you a good deal on my MochLava. It's going to be huge!"

"Thanks, but I like making mochas the old-fashioned way." Maddie tried to gracefully decline.

"You tasted it last weekend, right? There was enough for everyone—" He grimaced, as if remembering what had happened "—before … the unfortunate incident."

"Yes, we did." Suzanne's voice sounded extra cheery.

"What did you think?" he asked eagerly.

Maddie looked at her friend, wondering what she would say.

"It was certainly different," Suzanne said.

"Exactly!" He pointed a finger at her. "That's what everyone says. I've already got five coffee shops in Seattle signed up."

"That's great," Maddie said politely, wondering if the owners knew how bad his mocha beverage tasted. Or were the proprietors like Claudine in Estherville – whose notion of good taste was totally different to Maddie's and a lot of the other townsfolk?

"Sometimes I come in here for a cappuccino." He patted his belly. "Ellie makes a good one." He smiled genially at Ellie.

Ellie looked embarrassed, as if she wanted to escape. Before she could make an excuse, Fred called out:

"Hey, Rob, got a minute to talk?"

Maddie saw a harried looking man in his fifties stop in his tracks behind the counter, a resigned expression on his face. He beckoned to Fred.

"Gotta go, girls!" Fred bustled importantly toward the counter.

Ellie let out a sigh of relief.

"Do you know Fred?" Suzanne asked curiously.

Maddie glanced at Suzanne, hoping she would pick up the unspoken message that Maddie would need to take the lead on the questioning if she cast the Tell the Truth spell.

Once again, she fingered the notepaper in her hand. A calmness descended as she focused. She could see the words in her mind. Silently, she uttered them, whispering, "Show me," at the end.

"No." Ellie shook her head vehemently, then paused. "Not really."

"He seems to know you," Maddie observed.

Ellie fingered her ear, as if expecting to find an earring – like the ones she'd worn last weekend? "He's just a customer." She hesitated. "Once he said I reminded him of his granddaughter, which I thought was a nice thing to say.

But he mostly comes here to try and sell his mocha stuff to my boss."

"What does your boss think about it?" Maddie asked.

"Yesterday he said it was awful," Ellie replied. "But Fred keeps trying to sell it to him and … I don't know. I sort of admire his tenacity."

A deep knowing filled Maddie. The spell was working –Ellie was telling the truth right now!

"It's a shame Fred doesn't realize how bad it tastes," Suzanne remarked.

"Uh-huh." Ellie nodded.

"It was awful about Margot Wheeler – the judge – last Saturday," Maddie pressed.

"I felt terrible when we found out what happened." Ellie shivered. "You two found … her, didn't you?"

Maddie and Suzanne exchanged looks.

"Diana Swift found her first," Maddie admitted. "We were next on the scene."

"That must have been truly shocking." Ellie looked distressed.

Maddie wondered what would have happened if Ellie had been the first person to come across Margot. Would she have coped? Maybe it had been best that Maddie and Suzanne had arrived on the scene when they did.

"Congratulations on coming first after round one," Suzanne complimented her.

"Thanks." Ellie flushed. "I wasn't sure whether to enter the competition or not, but my boss encouraged me. And now I'm glad I did." Her pink cheeks deepened into red, and Maddie wondered if she was thinking of meeting Connor last Saturday.

"Oops!" Ellie checked her watch. "I've got to go. It's my lunch break soon."

"Sure." Suzanne smiled.

"Good luck for round two." Maddie smiled as well.

"Good luck to you too," Ellie replied, hurrying back to her barista station.

"Well," Suzanne said, lowering her voice and looking around the café to make sure nobody was paying any attention to their conversation. "What do you make of all that?"

"She was telling the truth," Maddie replied.

"To all of it?" Suzanne sat back in the chrome chair, a combination of relief and disappointment on her face.

"To everything we talked about after I cast the spell," Maddie replied. "Which was after you asked her if she knew Fred Beldon."

"Huh." Suzanne tapped her cup with her finger. "But don't you think it's weird that she knows Fred and he was the sponsor of the competition? Isn't that a conflict of interest?"

"Like the one Diana had when she discovered Margot was one of the members of her business club and was judging the competition?" Maddie asked dryly.

"Huh." Suzanne said again. "Although… Fred wasn't a judge, like Margot was. So even if Ellie knew ahead of time that Fred was going to be the sponsor for the competition, I don't see how that would give her an advantage, do you?"

"Not unless Fred had a quiet word with the judges and asked them to mark her higher."

"I can't imagine Margot agreeing to that." Suzanne's eyes widened as she realized what she'd said. "Do you think that's why she was killed? She refused to give someone higher scores?"

"If that's the reason, then I don't think Ellie is involved," Maddie replied. "I know she told us the truth about everything after I cast the spell."

"Or—" Suzanne looked excited. "Do you think she told the truth as far as she knew it? Like, what if she didn't know Fred wanted her to win the competition? What if Fred asked Margot to mark Ellie higher and she refused, so he killed her?"

"But we saw him in the café eating around the time of the murder," Maddie pointed out.

"Oh, yeah." Suzanne looked deflated.

"And why would Fred want Ellie to win the competition?" Maddie asked. "Because she reminds him of his granddaughter?"

"Hmm." Suzanne scrunched up her nose. "I think we'll have to ruminate some more on this aspect of the case."

Maddie giggled. "You sound just like Sherlock Holmes."

"Don't forget he always discovered the solution." Suzanne laughed too.

Maddie's stomach grumbled, reminding her it was time for lunch. "Where's this burger place you promised me?"

"Not far." Suzanne's eyes lit up. "You're right. We can talk more about this while we're munching on burgers."

They got up from the table, then Suzanne stopped in her tracks, Maddie nearly bumping into her.

"I can't believe we forgot to ask Ellie if Diana offered her the same job she offered you."

CHAPTER 8

Suzanne was right – they'd forgotten to ask Ellie that. But there had been other questions to ask, and Maddie had focused on casting the Tell the Truth spell as well.

Besides, as she'd already pointed out to Suzanne, they weren't professional investigators.

They walked out of the café, this time Maddie stopping in her tracks as she recognized the man heading in their direction.

"Suzanne," she hissed, nudging her friend.

"Oh, it's Connor." Suzanne stood stock still for a second, then moved forward, her lips turned up into a smile.

"Hi, Connor," she greeted him.

"Hey." He looked at her for a moment as if he wasn't quite sure where he knew her from, then recognition flickered across his face. "You're Maddie's friend – from the barista competition last weekend."

"That's right." Suzanne nodded.

"Hi, Connor." Maddie spoke.

He looked exactly the same as he had last Saturday – wearing light blue denim jeans and a plain black t-shirt, his forearms bare apart from the tattoos covering them.

"Hi, Maddie." He smiled, then nodded toward the café they'd just exited. "Have you checked out their coffee yet? Ellie's on today."

"Yep," Suzanne said. "And I had a wonderful mocha."

"I can see why she's leading the competition," Maddie said. "Her latte was great."

"Yeah, she has a real talent," Connor replied, rocking back on his heels. There was a faraway look on his face and Maddie wondered if he was thinking about Ellie's coffee – or Ellie herself.

"You must be good, too," Suzanne remarked. "You're coming second."

"Yeah." He grinned. "The competition was stiffer than I expected, though." He looked at Maddie in a way that made her wonder if he included her in the "stiff" competition.

155

"Well—" He checked his watch. "I've got to go. Ellie and I are having lunch next door." He gestured to a narrow storefront that advertised fresh sushi. "Hey, do you want to join us?"

"Thanks, but we were going to have lunch at a burger place near here that's supposed to be awesome." Suzanne dug out her phone and tapped the screen. "It's only a couple of blocks from here, isn't it?" She showed him the display.

"Oh yeah." Connor nodded. "That place has the best burgers. Mmm." For a second he looked like he'd rather have a burger than sushi for lunch. "Make sure you order the curly fries."

"Will do." Suzanne waved goodbye to him as he headed into the café. Maddie and Suzanne turned the corner.

"Don't you think they make a cute couple?" Suzanne mused.

"Ellie and Connor? Definitely."

"He's so big and tough looking and she's small and delicate, but they have coffee in common at least," Suzanne added.

They concentrated on finding the restaurant, Maddie silently cheering as it came into sight. Through the large glass window they could see that most of the tables were taken, but she spied two vacant ones in the back.

"Come on." She touched Suzanne's hand and hurried into the restaurant, where the aroma of grilled beef and fries filled the air.

The hostess seated them at a table for two, and left them to peruse the menu.

"I'm starving." Maddie scanned the menu, the sounds of diners talking to each other and rock music adding to the atmosphere. The wood paneled walls were covered in photos of cows in green pasture.

"I guessed." Suzanne giggled. "I am, too."

Maddie finally decided on a select your own burger, choosing a toasted brioche bun, large beef patty, bacon, lettuce, tomato, and barbecue sauce.

"We've got to get those curly fries Connor recommended," Suzanne reminded her.

The waitress came and took their order, arriving again in a couple of minutes with two glasses of freshly squeezed lemonade.

"Mmm," Maddie murmured, savoring the tart yet sweet beverage.

"I know." Suzanne sighed in pleasure. "I'm always telling myself I should make it at home, but I never get around to it."

When their burgers arrived, the large beef patties almost overwhelming the toasted buns, Maddie peered at Suzanne's plate. Her friend had ordered a burger with practically everything on it, even pickles, making it almost a mile high!

They didn't talk for a while, concentrating on their food instead. When almost all of the golden curly fries had vanished, Maddie leaned back in her wooden chair with a sigh of satisfaction.

"That was good."

"Uh-huh." Suzanne plucked the last fry from her plate and popped it into her mouth. "We have got to come here again," she said when she'd finished swallowing.

"My treat next time," Maddie offered.

"You're on." Suzanne grinned.

The waitress stopped by with the check, Suzanne flipping through her wallet for the right amount of cash.

Suddenly, a movement on the left side of the restaurant caught Maddie's attention. Was that …?

"Suzanne." She kept her voice low, her gaze darting to that side of the restaurant.

"What?" Suzanne looked up from her wallet, her brow crinkled. "I've got enough money, Mads."

"It's not that." Maddie jerked her head to the left. "It's Brad."

"OMG," Suzanne whispered. "What's he doing here?"

"Having lunch?"

"Yes, but … don't you think it's strange he's the third person from the competition we've seen today?"

"Not really," Maddie replied. "We specifically visited Ellie, and if Connor and Ellie are now seeing each other and they both work in nearby cafés, it's really not that surprising we bumped into Connor. But," she allowed, "I didn't expect to see Brad today."

"We've got to go and talk to him." Suzanne looked excited. She threw some cash on the table and scraped her chair back.

What are we going to say?" Maddie asked Suzanne as her friend strode over to the other side of the busy restaurant.

"Hi, Brad," Suzanne greeted the man, who looked just as grumpy as he had last Saturday. He wore a light blue shirt and black trousers – not the "lucky" shirt he'd worn then.

He looked up in surprise. A half full shot glass of golden liquid was on his table.

"Hi." He frowned. "Do I know you?"

"I'm Suzanne and this is Maddie. We met last Saturday at the barista competition."

"Oh, yeah." He nodded, then pointed a finger at Maddie, gun style. "You're coming third, right?"

"Yes," Maddie replied.

"Don't you two live hundreds of miles away?" His frown deepened. "What are you doing in the city?"

"We live *one* hundred miles away," Maddie told him. "In Estherville."

"So what are you doing here?" he persisted.

"Having lunch." Suzanne eyed his shot glass. "Just like you are. Except we enjoyed the freshly squeezed lemonade."

"I'm waiting for my order," he informed them, lifting the glass to his lips. He swallowed, satisfaction flickering across his face. "You can't beat a good bourbon – unless it's a good coffee."

"Are you looking forward to round two on Saturday?" Maddie asked politely.

"Yeah." A smile crossed his face. "Mochas are my specialty. How about you?"

"Maddie's great at making them," Suzanne said loyally.

"This is my first big competition," Maddie admitted. "Do you compete often?" She wondered if she should have saved the Tell the Truth spell for this man – but she'd had no idea that they were going to run into him today. Perhaps she should have cast a Coffee Vision spell before they left for Seattle.

"I used to but now I'm too busy running my coffee shop. It's four blocks away." He jerked his thumb to the right of the restaurant. "You should stop by some time and check me out."

A thought seemed to occur to him. "Hey, I'm looking for a new barista. One of mine just up and quit on me." He shook his head as if in disgust. "Want to audition?"

"No, thanks. I have my own coffee truck – with Suzanne."

"We've got our own coffee business."

Maddie and Suzanne spoke at the same time.

"Pity." He looked disappointed. "If you're good enough to come third so far, you might have been good enough to work for me."

"Um … thanks," Maddie finally said, unable to decide if he was complimenting her or just being obnoxious.

"Keep me in mind if you want a change of scene. I've got a good chance of winning on Saturday since I'll be wearing my lucky shirt, and then it's on to the nationals. I'm looking to expand my brand – before long I'll have a few more cafes around the city."

"Just like Diana Swift," Suzanne observed.

He snorted. "Fancy coffee for fancy people. Yeah, I heard about her idea last weekend. If you ask me, it will never get off the ground. People in this city want real coffee, not flavored this and flavored that."

Maddie and Suzanne exchanged a wide-eyed look. Brad's face had grown red with his vehemence. Maddie just hoped she and Suzanne didn't say anything else that would upset him further.

Saved by the waitress!

The same waitress who had served them earlier now bustled to the table, carrying a plate with a burger even bigger then Suzanne's, and French fries.

"We won't take up any more of your time," Maddie said as the waitress departed. "Good luck on Saturday."

"You too," he mumbled around a mouthful of fries.

Maddie and Suzanne hurried out of the restaurant.

"Did you see that?" Suzanne breathed as they reached the sidewalk. "He couldn't wait to start eating and stop talking to us."

"Maybe he was hungry." Maddie tried to be fair.

"I hope he doesn't win the final round." Suzanne frowned.

Maddie looked at her watch – it was two o'clock already.

"We better leave for Estherville – unless there's somewhere else you wanted to check out?"

"No." Suzanne shook her head. "After talking to him, the only thing I want to do is go home."

***

They arrived back in Estherville just after four o'clock. At the town square, Maddie jumped in the coffee truck and drove home, Suzanne right behind her.

On the drive back to Estherville, they'd decided that they should fill in Trixie on their outing to the city. Maddie hoped the Persian wouldn't be cross at being left at home.

"Trixie," Maddie called as she unlocked her front door, Suzanne standing behind her.

"Mrrow." Trixie walked down the hallway toward them, blinking sleepily at them.

"Did you sleep all day?" Suzanne asked. "Lucky you, Trix."

"Mrrow?" Trixie rubbed her face against Maddie's jean-clad legs, then stretched up against her knee.

Maddie crouched down and Trixie jumped into her arms.

"Ohh," Suzanne murmured. "That's so sweet."

Trixie turned her head toward Suzanne so she could pet her.

"I don't think she's mad – yet," Maddie said as she headed toward the kitchen, the cat still in her arms.

Trixie jumped onto the kitchen chair that Maddie privately labeled "Trixie's" and looked at them enquiringly.

"Wait 'til you hear what we found out today, Trix," Suzanne informed her.

"Want something to drink?" Maddie pulled out two mugs and looked at her friend.

"Maybe just some water." Suzanne patted her stomach. "I'm still full from that awesome burger and lemonade." She sighed in satisfaction. "And those curly fries."

"I know the feeling," Maddie admitted with a smile, coming back to the table with two glasses of water. "Would you like something, Trix?" She cast a glance at Trixie's bowl of kibble and water – there was still some dry food in it, and the water bowl looked good – Maddie had filled it that morning.

She swore Trixie had just shaken her head – ever so slightly. Was she imagining it? On the other hand, she could certainly believe that Trixie was able to answer her that way.

"Let me know if you do, Trixie," she said, sitting down at the table. "I've got some chicken in gravy for you."

"Mrrow." There was a pleased look on Trixie's face.

They told Trixie about Ellie's coffee, bumping into Connor, and then Brad after they'd had lunch at the burger place. At the mention of hamburgers, Trixie's ears pricked up and she seemed to pout when she realized they hadn't brought any home for her.

"Next time, Trix," Maddie promised.

Trixie answered with a grumbly "Mrrow" but seemed to continue listening to their conversation.

"I can't believe Brad had the nerve to offer you a barista "audition"." Suzanne shook her head.

"You can't expect him to offer a job to anyone without knowing how good they are at making coffee," Maddie said reasonably. "But I wasn't even tempted to try out – like I told him, we have our own coffee truck."

"Yeah." Suzanne's ponytail bounced as she nodded. "I don't know why anyone would want to work with him."

"Uh-huh." Maddie grimaced. "When he offered me that "audition" I couldn't help thinking back to what it was like working for Claudine."

"Yikes!" Suzanne shuddered. "Thank goodness we've got our own business and don't have to work for anyone else."

They smiled at each other in perfect agreement.

"Mrrow!" Trixie seemed to concur.

"And," Suzanne mused, "if Brad is such a skilled barista, why is he the last person to make the finals? He didn't seem bothered about it at all, did he?"

"Not if his abrasive personality is his normal one," Maddie replied.

"Maybe he's right and his mochas are super awesome," Suzanne continued. "But they'd have to be totally spectacular for him to beat you – and Ellie – and Connor – because the scores for round one are added to the round two scores. So how can he hope to finish in the top three?"

"I don't know. Unless he's bribed a judge?" Maddie said slowly. She didn't like to think a competitor would do that.

"OMG!" Suzanne hit the table with the palm of her hand. "What if he killed Margot Wheeler so he could put his own judge in – and what if that judge was able to convince the other two judges to mark him super high – that way he could win the competition and go on to the nationals!"

"Do you really think that's possible?" Maddie's tone was skeptical.

"Anything's possible when it comes to murder," Suzanne declared.

"But wouldn't it be obvious when the scores for round two are posted?" Maddie continued. "Surely it would look fishy if Brad suddenly has the highest scores from all three judges on the day of the final round? I can't believe the other competitors wouldn't say something about it, especially when the prize is one thousand dollars and an entry into the nationals."

"Good point." Suzanne looked a little deflated. "But I still think it's a decent theory."

"It's certainly a theory. Isn't it, Trixie?" Maddie looked at the cat.

"Mrrow." Maddie couldn't tell whether Trixie agreed with her or Suzanne.

"Didn't you think it was weird what Brad said about Diana Swift?" Suzanne continued, taking a sip of water.

"About how he doesn't think her chain of coffee shops will get off the ground? Definitely."

"She seemed so sure that they were going to be successful, and she offered you that job yesterday," Suzanne added.

"Yes, how can he be so certain?" Maddie furrowed her brow. "She told us she had the financing in place and that she's going to open the first store soon."

"Maybe he's just jealous," Suzanne considered. "He looks like he's in his forties and has one shop, while Diana seems to be thirty-something and is planning a whole chain of coffee shops. And she's beating him in the competition so far."

"Don't forget that Margot might have deliberately marked her higher than the other competitors," Maddie reminded her, "since they knew each other."

"Which doesn't give her a motive to kill Margot, does it?" Suzanne took another sip of water.

"No," Maddie agreed. "It doesn't seem to."

They sat at the kitchen table for a few more minutes, making plans to visit the burger place again in a couple of weeks – this time on a Sunday, their day off. Then Suzanne went home, reminding Maddie to practice making mochas for the final round on Saturday.

Maddie made mochas in the truck for an hour, mentally going over everything they'd seen and heard in Seattle that day, but she was no nearer a conclusion when she shut down the espresso machine. Mochas were one of her favorite beverages to make and drink, but right now, she was becoming a little tired of them.

CHAPTER 9

Friday. The day before the final round.

Maddie woke up, feeling slightly sick at the thought that tomorrow she would be competing for a spot in the national barista competition.

"Mrrow?" Trixie climbed on her chest, her face close to Maddie's.

"We have to get ready for work, Trix." Maddie smiled as Trixie tickled her cheek with her whiskers.

The Persian brushed her white whiskers against Maddie's face one more time, then jumped off the bed, scampering out of the room. Maddie knew what that meant – breakfast.

An hour later, Maddie drove to the town square, deliberately thinking about the latte Ellie had made her yesterday, and not about Luke coming to watch her compete tomorrow. She didn't need any extra pressure right now. She worried she was going to be a real basket case when they arrived in Seattle the next day.

"I've got a great idea!" Suzanne greeted Maddie as she parked the truck and hopped out.

"What's that?" Maddie smiled at her friend.

"Mrrow?" Trixie asked enquiringly from the window.

"You should get a massage from Ramon – to relax you for the competition tomorrow!" Suzanne looked pleased with herself.

Maddie felt even more nervous at the idea. She shook her head.

"I don't think that's such a good idea."

"Why not?"

"Because …" Maddie didn't know how to explain it. She just knew that doing something out of the ordinary today wasn't going to make her feel any better about the competition tomorrow.

"Are you sure you're not saying that because it will give you a chance to talk to Ramon?" she asked Suzanne.

"Well, there is that." Suzanne giggled. "But seriously, Mads, I thought a nice, relaxing massage with Ramon's soothing voice …" she looked dreamily into the

173

distance "… would do you a world of good."

"Maybe another time," Maddie replied, not wanting to hurt her friend's feelings. Suzanne raved about Ramon's magic hands, and his magic voice all the time, but Maddie wasn't sure whether massages were her thing. How much clothing did she have to take off? Suzanne assured her it was totally legit and professional but … maybe Maddie was too self-conscious.

"I bet Luke would give you a massage if you asked him," Suzanne said mischievously.

Maddie's face burned.

"Stop it!" She tapped Suzanne's arm.

"I think I'll call Luke right now and tell him you need to see him." Suzanne reached for her phone, a grin on her face.

Maddie lunged for the cell phone, desperate to get to it first. She knew – hoped – her friend was only joking, but she didn't think she and Luke were at that stage in their budding relationship.

"Lost something, girls?" Claudine's nasal voice made them freeze.

Maddie was aware Trixie watched all three of them with wide turquoise eyes, which slowly narrowed as she stared unblinkingly at Claudine.

"Why do you ask?" Suzanne asked coolly as she straightened up.

"Can we do something for you, Claudine?" Maddie asked politely, pushing back a strand of hair behind her ear. She was glad that none of their early morning customers had seen her and Suzanne wrestling.

"Just thought you'd like to know that your customers got what they needed at my coffee shop yesterday," Claudine informed them, a smug look on her face. "They were *so* disappointed that you were closed, but they soon cheered up when they tasted my coffee."

"As if," Suzanne muttered under her breath.

"Nothing wrong I hope, Maddie?" Claudine peered at them through the serving window.

"Everything is wonderful, Claudine," Maddie told her, forcing a big smile on her face. She would not let this woman see how nervous she felt about tomorrow.

175

"We had an awesome day in Seattle yesterday," Suzanne declared. "The most amazing lunch, the most amazing coffee, and the most amazing friend to share it with." She wrapped her arm around Maddie's waist, and Maddie returned the gesture.

"Mrrow!" Trixie joined in, acting as if she had been to Seattle with them.

"Hmmph." Claudine's black eyebrows lowered. "Well, if that's how you treat your business …"

"Our business is better than ever," Suzanne told her. "And after tomorrow – well, the sky's the limit."

"What are you talking about?" Claudine glowered at them.

"It's the final round tomorrow," Suzanne replied. "And Maddie's coming third right now. And you know what the first prize is, don't you, Claudine? One thousand dollars and an entry into the nationals."

For a second, Claudine looked like she was going to explode.

"Hmmph." Claudine growled, turning on her heel and striding back to her café.

"You shouldn't bait her like that, Suzanne."

"She deserved it," Suzanne replied. "I hate how she comes over here and acts as if her coffee is better than ours."

"We know it's not, and a lot of locals know it's not either," Maddie pointed out. "And if some of our customers went to her café yesterday, it was probably because they were so desperate for caffeine they didn't care what it tasted like."

"I know. You're right." Suzanne sighed. "She just gets me all steamed up!"

"Maybe *you* should book a massage with Ramon." Maddie giggled.

"But that might make me feel even steamier!" Suzanne laughed, her face flushing.

"Thank goodness you're open, Maddie." A middle-aged businessman, who was one of their regulars, looked relieved. "I'll have a large latte with an extra shot. Yesterday I went to Claudine's for an afternoon caffeine fix and—" he shuddered. "I would have been

177

better off making instant coffee in the office."

"Coming right up." Maddie smiled at him, and set to work at the machine, the sound of hissing and burring filling the small truck.

"Yay!" Suzanne said under her breath as she took their customer's money.

"Mrrow." Trixie waved a paw at their customer.

"Hi, Trixie." He grinned at her.

After that, they had a never-ending stream of customers until mid-morning, some of them asking if Maddie and Suzanne were going to be there for the rest of the day.

"You called it," Suzanne told Maddie as they finally got to sit down for a few minutes, their last customer holding her coffee in one hand and pushing her baby's pram with the other. "Business will be back to usual for Claudine today – way down on yesterday."

"Mmm." Maddie took a sip of bottled water. She didn't think she needed the heightened effects of caffeine today. "Claudine's still in business though, so she must have some customers who like her coffee – or her pastries."

"Unless she only gets people from out of town." Suzanne shrugged. "Or aliens from out of space." She giggled.

Maddie allowed herself to join in the silliness. Even Trixie looked like she was enjoying the joke.

"Hello, Maddie and Suzanne." Ramon's Spanish accent quickly sobered them.

"Hi, Ramon." Suzanne jumped off the stool and bounced to the serving window.

"Hi, Ramon." Maddie smiled and walked the two steps to join Suzanne.

"Mrrow." Trixie sat up straight on her stool and waved a paw at him, tilting her head on her side flirtatiously.

"How are you, Trixie?" Ramon asked the cat.

"Mrrow," Trixie chirped at him.

Maddie could have sworn Trixie would have batted her eyelashes at him if she had any.

"I just wanted to stop by and wish you luck for tomorrow, Maddie," Ramon told her, his molten brown eyes radiating sincerity.

"Thanks." Maddie took in a breath. She suddenly wondered if Ramon had ever been on the cover of a romance novel.

"Have they discovered who the murderer is?" he asked.

"Nope." Suzanne's ponytail swished as she shook her head.

"If they have, they haven't informed us," Maddie amended.

"That is too bad," he replied. "You and Suzanne must tell me all about it on Monday. I hope you win, Maddie."

"She's definitely got a good chance," Suzanne said.

Ramon smiled – a smile that would probably cause hearts to flutter around the world. "I will be thinking of both of you. You and Suzanne must be careful while you are in the city – especially if the killer is still out there."

"We will be," Suzanne promised.

"Yes," Maddie replied, noticing the special smile Suzanne gave the Spaniard. A smile that seemed to be returned.

Ramon left without ordering a coffee, explaining he would make himself one at his salon, so Maddie wouldn't be overtaxed the day before the final round.

"He is so thoughtful," Suzanne gushed as she watched him stride across the town square to his storefront.

"Definitely," Maddie agreed, knowing that while she could admire the sexy Spaniard, her heart belonged to Luke.

A few customers snagged their attention, then they had a few minutes reprieve.

"I must make more health balls." Suzanne looked guiltily at the empty platter. "I've only made one batch all week!"

"We've been busy," Maddie soothed. "And if you made some now, we'd have to sell them all today, since we won't be open tomorrow."

"We can take the leftovers with us tomorrow to nibble on." Suzanne grinned, whipping out her phone and beginning to type a list of ingredients.

"Hello, Maddie." Detective Edgewater appeared in front of the serving window.

"Hi, Detective Edgewater."

"Have you got any news for us?" Suzanne looked up eagerly from her shopping list.

"What news would that be?" the detective teased. "Or are you talking about the judge who was murdered?" He sobered.

"You know we are." Suzanne hurried over to the window.

"I'm afraid in that case I don't have anything for you." The detective shook his head. "The murder is still unsolved. That's why I stopped by – as well as for a large vanilla cappuccino."

"Coming right up." Maddie set to work at the espresso machine.

"Mrrow." Trixie greeted the detective.

"Hello, Trixie," he replied. "You'll make sure these two behave themselves, won't you? And not get mixed up in any danger?"

"Mrrow." Trixie sat up straighter on her stool as if she were saying, "Yes."

"I'm leaving Trixie with my mother tomorrow," Maddie informed him as she handed him his coffee.

"Good idea." He took a sip, a smile spreading across his face. "I hope you win tomorrow, Maddie. You certainly deserve to."

"Thanks, Detective Edgewater," she replied.

"The final round tomorrow is mochas," Suzanne told him. "Maddie's been practicing all week."

Maddie hoped she didn't look guilty as she remembered she hadn't practiced *every* day.

"Next time I'll order a mocha," he promised. "And if you win tomorrow, you'll be able to call them "award winning"."

"That's my – our – plan!" Suzanne grinned. "We'll definitely do that, Mads."

Maddie just hoped everyone wouldn't be disappointed if she didn't win tomorrow – she might be talented as a barista and make the best coffee in the small town of Estherville, but did that mean she was good enough to win the competition?

CHAPTER 10

"Thanks, Mom." Maddie kissed her mother's cheek as she and Suzanne handed her all of Trixie's essentials for twenty-four hours.

"Mrrow." Trixie pouted as she inspected her water bowl, food dish, dry food and wet food, litter tray, and the new toy Maddie had bought on the way home from work yesterday to assuage her guilty conscience at leaving Trixie with her mother for the day – an orange hessian mouse.

What if the murderer struck again today at the barista competition? She and Suzanne might be required to stay overnight in Seattle again, and Maddie wanted to make sure Trixie was being cared for if that happened.

"I'm sure Trixie will be fine," Maddie's mother told her. "She was so well behaved last weekend, weren't you, Trixie?"

"Mrrow." Trixie blinked up at Maddie's mother – Trixie's

grandmother? Maddie thought fleetingly – looking as if a frozen liver ice cube would *not* melt in her mouth.

"See?" Maddie's mother looked pleased. "And I even bought her a blanket – so she can curl up in the armchair in the living room and be all nice and cozy." Mrs. Goodwell held up a fluffy pink blanket. "The color compliments her fur."

"Oh, Mom." Maddie couldn't help smiling. Trixie had certainly cast a spell over her mother last weekend.

"Mrrow." Trixie looked up at Mrs. Goodwell, as if saying thank you, a pleased expression on her face.

"Why don't we try it out, Trixie?" Maddie's mother headed toward the living room, Trixie trotting behind her.

Maddie and Suzanne watched as Mrs. Goodwell spread the blanket on the armchair, encouraging Trixie to hop up.

The Persian did so, turning around in a circle, then settling down after giving the blanket a couple of experimental kneads.

"She'll be as good as gold," Maddie's mother declared, smiling at the fluffy white cat.

"We should be back by tonight," Maddie told Trixie, stroking her soft fur.

"Mrrow." Trixie blinked at her, as if saying, "Good luck", then snuggled into the blanket.

Maddie wondered at Trixie's calm acceptance that she would be spending the day with Maddie's mom.

"I'm sure she'd rather be with you – us," Suzanne told her as they headed back to Maddie's car.

"I think she's got Mom wrapped around her little paw," Maddie said wryly.

An image flashed through Maddie's mind of her and Trixie snuggled up on the sofa, *Wytchcraft for the Chosen* open on Maddie's lap. She stopped walking so suddenly that Suzanne almost cannoned into her.

Had Trixie just communicated telepathically with her? The feelings that the image evoked were warm, fuzzy, feel good ones. Had her cat wanted to reassure her that Maddie was still her number one person?

"What is it?" Suzanne placed a hand over her chest.

"Sorry. Nothing … bad, anyway." Maddie smiled, wanting to share the moment with her friend, but also wanting to keep it as a private moment between her and Trixie.

"Come on," Suzanne urged. "We've got to pick up Luke and get to the hotel. You don't want to be late."

At the mention of Seattle, Maddie's nerves returned full force. They got in her car and drove to Luke's house. Although she'd been dating him for a few weeks, she hadn't been invited over – yet.

Suzanne directed her and in a few minutes they parked outside a small Craftsman style house sporting cedar shingles and attractive gray stone. His tan SUV was in the driveway.

Maddie unclenched her fingers from the steering wheel. Maybe Luke coming with them wasn't such a good idea. But it was too late now. How much more nervous could she get, anyway?

Stage fright.

She bit her lip at the thought of freezing in front of the judges and her fellow competitors. She would be *so* embarrassed.

"Are you okay?" Suzanne touched her arm.

"No – yes." Maddie forced a smile.

"You're going to be fine," Suzanne encouraged her. "You're an awesome barista, and you're coming third right now. You've beaten a lot of competitors already. It would be great if you win today, but if you don't, we've still got the truck to open on Monday and all our customers to serve. They'll be glad that you're there, giving them the best coffee ever."

"Thanks." A tight knot of tension eased inside her. "You're the best."

"So are you. And my brother seems to think so, too." A mischievous look crossed Suzanne's face as she looked out of the passenger window.

Luke crossed his front lawn and headed toward the car, a smile on his face. He wore pressed jeans and an indigo shirt.

Instantly, butterflies skyrocketed in her stomach.

"I think we should take your car, Luke." Suzanne hopped out and spoke to her brother.

"Sure," Luke said easily, his gaze fixed on Maddie.

"Hi," Maddie said softly, getting out of the vehicle.

"Hi," Luke replied. The two of them stood staring at each other across the roof of the car.

Suzanne cleared her throat. "I think we should get going now. We don't want to be late," she added in a louder voice, as if to snag their attention.

"Oh – yeah." Luke seemed to focus on his sister's words at last.

Maddie joined the two of them, Luke steering her to the passenger side of his SUV.

"I'll sit in the back," Suzanne offered with a grin.

"Good idea." Luke smiled at his sister, opening the car doors for both girls.

"Thank you," Maddie said softly as she climbed into the SUV. It was higher off the ground than her white compact car.

Suzanne closed her door, and Maddie did likewise, as Luke got in and started the engine.

Maddie's hands trembled as she buckled her seatbelt. Right now, she didn't know whether it was from the close proximity to Luke, even with Suzanne acting as chaperone, or the fact that in three hours she would be attempting to make the best mocha of her life. Or maybe both!

The drive to Seattle went smoothly. Although Maddie was conscious – way too conscious – of Luke's presence beside her, his faint scent of lemony citrus, and the way he drove – safely but not like a little old lady – the trip turned out to be fun. They finally agreed on a pop rock station, turning down the volume to background music so they could easily talk to each other.

When they reached the outskirts of the city, Suzanne directed him to the hotel. Luke parked in the visitor garage, and Maddie took a deep breath as she unbuckled her seat belt. One hour to go.

"I have to register," Maddie stated, glad that her voice sounded fairly normal.

"No worries," Luke replied, giving her a smile.

They headed into the hotel, Maddie and Suzanne looking around for a notice indicating the location of the competition.

"There it is!" Suzanne pointed to a discreet sign telling them that the competition would be held next to the ballroom.

"I'm glad it's not the ballroom." Maddie gave Suzanne a heartfelt look. That would seem like bad luck – or even déjà vu – if the killer struck again.

Maddie and Suzanne looked at each other with wide eyes, as if they'd just had the same thought.

"What are you two thinking?" Luke asked.

"I don't think you want to know," Suzanne said.

"Maddie?" Luke turned to her, a questioning look on his face.

"Um … what Suzanne said," Maddie mumbled.

"The police haven't caught the killer yet," Suzanne told her brother.

"And the organizers think it's a good idea to hold the competition here again?" He frowned.

"I'm sure there'll be a police presence," Suzanne told him.

"I hope so," Maddie murmured.

They walked down the well-lit hallway to the ballroom. Maddie spied a couple of people further down, and gestured to Luke and Suzanne.

A table was set up outside the smaller conference room next to the ballroom, where Detective Rawson had interviewed them last week. A clerk sat there, surrounded by paperwork.

Maddie registered, pinning her badge with the number three to her peach top. She wondered if all the finalists' badges indicated their ranking in the competition so far.

"Look." Suzanne nudged her. "Police presence." A police officer came out of the conference room and walked down the hallway.

Maddie gave her a relieved smile.

A few minutes later, the doors were opened by the registration clerk.

"I guess that means we can go in," Maddie remarked.

"Come on!" Suzanne headed inside.

Maddie and Luke followed, sharing a smile at Suzanne's eagerness.

The walls were painted vanilla and the carpet was a rosy beige hue. There were rows of black plastic chairs for the audience, just like last week in the ballroom, and eight espresso stations at the front of the room. To the left was a long table which Maddie assumed was for the judges – again, just like last week.

To her relief, there was not a vat of mocha – not yet, anyway.

As soon as they entered, more people trickled in.

"Look." Suzanne nudged her. "There's Diana."

"And Ellie and Connor," Maddie added, pleased to see that they walked in together. She wondered if they were officially an item or if one week was too soon.

She peeked at Luke. Were *they* officially an item? Nothing had been said yet – they hadn't even kissed! Maddie filed the thought away to the back of her mind. Right now, she needed to focus on the competition.

"Brad," she murmured to Suzanne as the man entered the room, a confident expression on his face. Just like last week, he wore a gray shirt with mid-blue buttons rimmed in gold and black trousers. His "lucky" shirt.

"Oh, Maddie!" Ellie hurried over to her, Connor following. "I've been offered a new job!"

"Really?" Maddie asked, wondering if it had been the same one she'd been offered by Diana. She noticed that Ellie wore her sister's fairy earrings again.

"It sounds really exciting." Ellie looked over at Diana. "Diana offered it to me yesterday but I haven't made up my mind yet, though."

"I've been telling her she can do it," Connor said, looking encouragingly at Ellie. "The pay is better than what she's making now."

"And I love the idea of coming up with new speciality drinks." Ellie smiled, then her face fell. "But I don't know about training the other baristas."

Maddie thought Ellie seemed a little less shy than last Saturday, and wondered if it was her new friendship with Connor that had made a difference.

"Wouldn't it be cool if Diana offered both of you jobs?" Suzanne mused. "Connor could handle the training and you could concentrate on roasting and creating new drinks and all the things you like doing."

"How do you know the job includes roasting the beans?" Ellie furrowed her brow.

"Diana offered me the job on Wednesday." Maddie decided she should be honest.

"And Maddie turned it down," Suzanne added.

Luke nodded. Maddie had told him about it on their Wednesday night date.

"Really?" Ellie looked disappointed – and perplexed.

"I realized it wasn't what I wanted," Maddie replied. "And I think the commute to Seattle every day would have killed me."

Connor nodded as if in understanding.

"But I'm sure it's a great job," Maddie added.

"It sounds like it," Connor said. He wrapped an arm around Ellie's shoulder. "But it's up to Ellie to decide if it's right for her."

Maddie smiled at the couple, thinking Suzanne had been right – they did seem well suited, even though on the surface they might appear a bit of a mis-match.

Maddie remembered what Brad had said to them on Thursday, when they'd bumped into him at the burger place.

"Diana has everything ready to go with her flagship store, doesn't she?" she asked.

"Yes." Ellie nodded. "She even showed me the space – it's only a few blocks from where I'm working now."

"And she should be ready to open next month," Connor added.

"That's great." Maddie smiled. That information was totally different to what Brad had told them.

"Have you thought some more about my offer, Ellie?" Diana joined their little group.

"Hi, Diana," Ellie said shyly. "Um … I'm still thinking about it."

"Hello, Maddie and Suzanne." Diana smiled at them.

"Hi," they chorused, returning her smile.

Maddie belatedly realized she hadn't introduced Luke.

Suzanne must have had the same thought because she said, "This is my brother Luke."

Maddie looked at her gratefully. How would she have introduced him? Her longtime crush? – too embarrassing! The guy she'd been dating for a few weeks? Suzanne's brother? But if she only said that, what would have Luke thought? Or maybe she could have just said, "This is Luke." She nodded to herself. She'd have to remember that for next time – until she knew for sure that they were officially an item.

A woman in her sixties walked into the room, dressed in a green paisley designer suit. Her gray hair was worn in a soft bob, and she looked professional but approachable.

"Who's that?" Suzanne whispered.

The rest of them shrugged in an "I don't know" manner, but they all watched as the newcomer made her way to the judge's table.

The two male judges from last week appeared in the doorway, scanning the room.

"Hello, everyone!" The portly male judge called out. "Competitors, please find a station. Members of the audience, please find a seat. We will start shortly."

Maddie noticed the two judges greeting the sixty-something woman at the judge's table. Was she the new judge?

She risked a glance at Diana. Did she know the female judge? Were they both members of the business club?

But Maddie couldn't discern a hint of recognition on Diana's face as she gazed at the newcomer.

Maddie waved goodbye to Suzanne and Luke, following the others to the espresso stations. The rest of the competitors had already chosen a station, and she found herself next to Brad and Diana. Not quite déjà vu. She suddenly realized that she hadn't spotted Fred Beldon in the room, or his vat of mocha – thank goodness. She wondered if he was going to make an appearance today given what had happened last weekend.

The two male judges checked each contestant off their list, making sure their number badge was consistent with the rest of their details.

"You will have five minutes to make three mochas," the portly male judge announced. "Get your beans ready, please."

Maddie had already placed her beans and chocolate powder on her workspace, and noticed Brad and Diana Swift had as well.

"Your time starts now." A bell tinkled.

Maddie closed her eyes, trying to focus on the task in hand. She heard burring and grinding from her neighbors, but tuned it out, instead concentrating on what she needed to do.

An image popped into her head of the three judges, including the new female judge, complimenting her on her mocha. She frowned. She knew she hadn't been thinking about that – she'd been busy grinding her beans, focusing on getting the grind just right.

Had it been Trixie?

Warmth flooded her at the idea that her familiar had been thinking of her at a crucial time. She didn't want to let herself down – or Trixie. Or Suzanne – or Luke.

Maddie set to work with renewed vigor, determined to make the best mocha ever.

When the buzzer sounded, signaling the end of the round, Maddie stepped back, looking at the three mochas she'd just finished making, thick with foam. Satisfaction stole through her. She just hoped they tasted as good as they looked.

"Step back from your stations, please." The portly male judge clapped his hands.

Maddie noticed that Brad had continued to pour his third mocha after the buzzer went off. He stepped back from the machine, a smug look on his face.

"They've never tasted anything like mine," he told Maddie.

His mochas looked good, Maddie had to admit. The foam looked decent, and the cocoa color, as well as the chocolatey coffee aroma, encouraged her to try one right away. But even if his mochas were the best in the room, would he earn enough points to become the overall winner considering he was currently in eighth place?

The three judges strolled around the stations, tasting each mocha and making notes on their clipboard.

Maddie watched them taste Brad's mocha, approval flitting across their faces as they talked to each other in hushed tones, and jotted notes on their clipboards.

Maddie was next.

The female judge nodded to her, and took a sip of mocha. She took another – and another, then smiled at Maddie.

"Excellent."

"Thank you," Maddie murmured, excited butterflies zooming around in her stomach. Would the two male judges have the same opinion?

The portly judge tasted her mocha, smiling at her. He wrote something down on his clipboard, then addressed her.

"Where do you work—" he peered at her number badge and then at the clipboard – "Ms. Goodwell?"

"I run a coffee truck in Estherville with my friend." When he looked like he didn't know where Estherville was, she elaborated, "One hundred miles away."

"The people of Estherville are very lucky." He nodded to her, then went on to sample Diana's entry.

Maddie grinned, unable to help herself. Even if she didn't win, it was wonderful to have her barista skills acknowledged by the judges.

The second male judge beamed at her after he tasted her mocha, wrote something on his clipboard, then tested Diana's offering.

"Yours look pretty good," Brad told Maddie, still looking smug. "Let me know if you change your mind about auditioning for me."

"Um … thanks." She didn't wish to be rude.

"They loved my mochas," he continued. "Once I win the nationals I'll be able to write my own ticket. That means I'll be able to start up my new business importing and roasting beans and selling them to all the coffee houses in the city."

"That sounds impressive," Maddie replied. Was winning the nationals such a career boost?

"I'll have no problems getting investors," he continued. "And I'll still have my own coffee shop – I might even expand there as well. This competition is just the start."

Maddie felt totally unambitious compared to him, and also Diana. The judges had moved on to Ellie, who fidgeted as they tasted her mochas.

Was it so bad to enjoy being a small-town barista with her own coffee truck and having fun working with Suzanne and Trixie? Maddie didn't think so – right now, she knew deep down inside that the path she was on was the right one for her.

Besides, she had *Wytchcraft for the Chosen* to focus on as well if the book's prediction was correct, and she was now coming into her full powers as a witch, however slowly.

She hadn't even had a chance to try casting the How to Move an Object spell.

The portly male judge clapped his hands to attract everyone's attention.

"We will now tabulate the scores." He smiled at the competitors. "We'll try to be as quick as possible, but we must be accurate. In half an hour or so, we'll announce the winner. Until then, feel free to leave your station. After the announcement, the scores will be posted outside."

Déjà vu.

Except this time, they weren't in the ballroom where the murder had taken place, they were in the smaller room next door.

The other competitors threaded their way toward the audience. Maddie followed.

"How did you go?" Connor asked as he fell into step beside her, Ellie on his other side.

"I'm not sure," Maddie said cautiously. She didn't want to boast – what if she wasn't good enough to win? "I think they liked my mochas, though."

"Yeah." He nodded. "They said they enjoyed mine, but they also said that to Ellie."

"Yes." Ellie touched one of her fairy earrings, as if for extra luck.

"You were awesome, Maddie!" Suzanne rushed up to her, Luke following.

"Thanks." She smiled at her friend's enthusiasm, her gaze meeting Luke's.

"Definitely." He cleared his throat, a warm expression in his green eyes.

"Here's my card." Brad came up to their group, pressing a business card into Maddie's hand. "If you ever decide to audition for me ..." He winked, then strode over to another competitor, clearly pleased with his performance.

"Yuck." Suzanne made a face. "As if you'd want to do *that*."

"I know," Maddie murmured.

"He's a good barista," Connor said, "but he does have a tendency to rub people the wrong way."

All four of them looked at him.

"When you've been working in the business for a while in Seattle, you tend to run into the same people," he told them.

Ellie nodded, and Maddie remembered how Fred Beldon, the mocha sponsor, was one of the ethereal girl's customers – or one of her boss's customers.

"I guess," Maddie said thoughtfully.

"What should we do now?" Suzanne checked her watch. "Do we have time to go to the hotel coffee shop before they announce the winner?"

After the stress of competing, the last thing Maddie wanted was to drink coffee. Maybe she'd order a soothing cup of tea – something she rarely drank unless she was in the mood.

"It looks like they've made their decision already." Luke motioned in the direction of the judge's table.

The three judges were in a huddle, looking at a clipboard and nodding to each other. Then the female judge stood.

"May I have everyone's attention?" She clapped her hands for effect. "We are now ready to announce the winner."

"Am I late?" Fred Beldon bustled into the room, the door swinging behind him. He hurried over to the judge's table, looking at them expectantly.

The portly male judge stood to greet him. "No, you're not late. In fact, you have perfect timing." The expression on his face suggested otherwise, though.

Did that mean he didn't approve of Fred Beldon's mocha beverage – MochLava – either?

"As the sponsor of this competition, I think it's only fitting that I award the prizes," Fred stated.

"Quite so," the trim male judge said. "But we weren't sure if you were coming today, since you weren't here at the beginning of the final round and—" he looked at his watch "—we've only booked this room for a certain amount of time. Which is why we were going to announce the winners now and wrap up the competition."

"Who won?" Fred asked.

The female judge put a finger to her lips, then turned around her clipboard, showing the information to Fred.

"Let's announce the winner!" Fred grinned.

An excited buzz of conversation swept the room.

"Competitors, please come back to your stations," the female judge called out.

Maddie followed Ellie and Connor back to the espresso stands. She looked around at the competitor's area, noting that all the entrants were there, looking either confident (Brad) or apprehensive (Ellie). She wasn't sure about the expression on her own face – probably two-thirds nervous and one-third hopeful.

The female judge gestured for silence as the audience members took their seats once more.

Fred Beldon held up the clipboard, looking very important.

"In third place – Connor from Snag Coffee in Seattle," he stated.

The audience members applauded. Maddie twisted around to see Connor's expression. He looked pleased but also a little disappointed. That was understandable – she remembered him telling her last weekend that the first prize of one thousand dollars would come in handy.

"In second place – Maddie from Brewed from the Bean in Estherville."

"Yay!" Suzanne jumped up, applauding wildly. Luke also stood, a big grin on his face.

A wave of relief swept over her. She hadn't embarrassed herself. Second place was pretty good, especially with the level of competition. But she couldn't help feeling a little disappointed that she hadn't come first.

"And in first place …" Fred Beldon paused for dramatic effect "… Ellie from Hannon's in Seattle."

Ellie looked stunned, blinking as if in shock. Maddie watched her touch one of her fairy earrings and wondered if she was thanking the fairies for her win – that is, if fairies actually existed.

Connor congratulated Ellie by hugging her, causing an adorable blush to cover her cheeks.

Connor, Maddie, and Ellie walked over to the judge's table to receive their prizes. In Connor and Maddie's case, it was a gilt-edged certificate, but Ellie received a small gold trophy and a check for one thousand dollars.

Fred Beldon looked pleased as he handed Ellie her prizes. Maddie thought Ellie seemed embarrassed at the attention – or was it due to the fact that Fred was congratulating her?

Her mind flashed back to the day she and Suzanne visited her at the Seattle café. Ellie had claimed that Fred was just a customer, but was there more to it than that? Could Ellie possibly be involved in the murder of Margot Wheeler?

As the three of them walked back to their stations, Maddie noticed that Diana looked disappointed, but she congratulated them all graciously.

Brad's jaw pulsed, as if he couldn't believe he hadn't won.

"Rigged," he gritted. "It's got to be rigged." He marched over to the judge's table, planting his hands on the table and leaning in to speak to all three judges – and Fred Beldon.

Audience members came over to the competitors, all of them talking at once and creating a loud buzz of conversation.

"OMG, Maddie!" Suzanne hugged her, her face alight with excitement. "You came second!"

"You're not disappointed I didn't win?" Maddie looked first at Suzanne, and then Luke.

"Of course not! Well, not really," Suzanne amended. "You beat out Connor and Diana – and Brad. That's great going."

"I'm proud of you, Maddie," Luke told her, causing her to blush.

"Besides," Suzanne went on, "if you won you'd have to compete in the nationals and I know you might have been a *little* stressed about competing today – and last weekend. You might be a huge jangly ball of nerves if you had to do it all over again for an even bigger competition."

Maddie nodded, glad that her friend understood her so well.

An image appeared in her mind, of Trixie nestling in her arms, purring, and looking happy. Was that her cat's way of congratulating her?

She smiled, trying to hold onto the vision, but it slowly disappeared.

"Maddie?" Suzanne waved a hand in front of her face.

"What?" Maddie blinked, the room coming into focus.

"Detective Edgewater and Detective Rawson are here."

"Where?" Maddie frowned, scanning the room. The warm feelings Trixie's image had evoked faded as she searched for the two investigators.

"Over there." Luke gestured to the back row of chairs intended for the audience. The detectives were talking to each other and looking at a notepad.

"I didn't notice them when we got here, did you?" Maddie asked.

"Nope." Suzanne shook her head. "They must have arrived during the final round."

"I hope this means they've discovered who the killer is," Luke remarked.

Out of the corner of her eye, Maddie noticed Brad stomping to his espresso station and grabbing his things. He did not look happy.

"Look." Maddie nudged Suzanne.

"Yikes," Suzanne whispered. "After all his bragging, he didn't even make it in the top three. I wonder where he placed."

"What are you two whispering about?" Luke asked curiously.

"Nothing," Maddie and Suzanne chorused. Maddie didn't know how Luke would feel about the fact that she and Suzanne had done a little snooping, or in Suzanne's words, keeping their eyes and ears open.

"The scores will be posted outside," the female judge raised her voice so everyone could hear her. "Congratulations to the winners, and thank you to everyone who entered. We hope that next year's competition will be even bigger and better. And now, we will have a minute's silence for Margot Wheeler, who died tragically last week in the course of her involvement in this year's competition."

Maddie bowed her head, noticing Suzanne and Luke did likewise. If only she and Suzanne had found out who killed Margot – but surely the detective would be able to figure it out? She crinkled her brow. Why was Detective Edgewater here? This wasn't his case – unless he was in Seattle visiting his nephew and had decided to accompany him to the scene of the crime – well, almost the scene of the crime since the murder had taken place in the next room.

The minute of silence was over. People began talking quietly. Maddie opened her eyes, and noticed Detective Edgewater making his way over to her.

"Congratulations, Maddie." He smiled at her.

"Thank you," she replied.

"What are you doing here, Detective Edgewater?" Suzanne asked innocently.

He chuckled. "Visiting my nephew – and since he had to be here, I thought I'd tag along and watch the competition." He looked curiously at Luke.

Maddie's theory was correct!

"This is my brother, Luke," Suzanne introduced them.

The two men shook hands.

"I expect you three will be on your way home now," Detective Edgewater said in an encouraging tone.

"I expect so," Suzanne replied. "Once we get something to eat at the coffee shop. I'm starving!"

"Just be careful," he told them. "The killer is still on the loose."

"Do you have any leads?" Luke asked.

"All I can say is that the Seattle police are working on it," the detective told them. "Congratulations again, Maddie."

"Thank you," Maddie replied, glancing at her certificate. It did look quite impressive. All she wanted to do was go

home and snuggle on the sofa with Trixie
and tell her about today. She fleetingly
wondered if one day she'd be snuggling
on the sofa with Luke, too.

"Let's check out the scores on the way
to the coffee shop," Suzanne suggested.

"Good idea," Luke replied.

They said goodbye to Detective
Edgewater and made their way toward
the exit. Ahead of them, Brad was talking
sullenly to another competitor, one
Maddie hadn't met.

"I guess your "lucky" shirt wasn't
lucky enough," the other competitor
teased Brad. "Tough luck, man."

"I still say it was rigged." Brad looked
ferocious. "I complained to the judges but
they don't care." He looked like he
wanted to punch something. Swiveling
on his heel, he glanced at Maddie, his
angry glare resting on her, forcing her to
take a step back.

Maddie remembered Brad boasting
about his "lucky" shirt last weekend at
the beginning of round one. She squinted
at the buttons on his gray "lucky" shirt,
focusing on the gold rimmed edging
around the circles of mid-blue.

Had there been something about his shirt that caught her attention last weekend? She frowned, attempting to concentrate, but the only thing she could think of was how abrasive the man seemed.

They edged their way around the two men, Maddie glad to get away from Brad.

"Come on," Suzanne urged, hurrying over to the white sheet of paper affixed to the wall outside. "I want to see the scores."

Maddie scanned the scoresheet, first for her score, and then for the other competitors. It seemed that the new female judge marked quite evenly, and on par with the two male judges – quite a change from the way Margot scored the competitors last weekend.

She noticed that Diana had come fourth and that the female judge had given her a lower score than Maddie, Ellie, and Connor – so maybe the two women didn't know each other –unlike Margot and Diana.

Brad had snagged fifth place, an improvement on his previous eighth place ranking. Maybe he was right about his mochas being excellent.

"You were so close, Maddie," Suzanne remarked, tapping the score sheet with her finger. "You were only three points behind Ellie."

"And Connor was only one point behind you," Luke added.

Maddie took one last look at the scores. If Ellie's barista skills were better than hers, then she deserved to win, as long as she hadn't been involved with the murder.

Connor and Ellie came out of the room, talking animatedly to each other, Ellie clutching her trophy. They smiled and waved to Maddie, Suzanne, and Luke, then headed down the hallway.

"I think Suzanne's idea of going to the coffee shop is a good one," Luke said. "We can have a late lunch there and then go home."

"Good idea," Maddie replied, deciding to focus on something more pleasant that the killer's identity. She realized with a start that her stomach had started to grumble. "Anything except coffee!"

CHAPTER 11

Luke found them a table at the hotel café and they perused the menu. Maddie finally decided on a turkey panini, Suzanne declaring she would have the same, and Luke ordered a cheeseburger and fries.

"I think we should have gone to that "authentic" burger place," Suzanne said after they'd ordered. "Those burgers and curly fries were amazing."

"Don't forget the freshly squeezed lemonade," Maddie added.

"Now you tell me." Luke mock-groaned.

"But it would have taken us too long to get there," Suzanne continued. "Maddie and I are going there again in a couple of weeks – want to come with?"

"I'd love to." Luke's gaze held Maddie's for a long moment, causing her to blush.

Maybe she should have a little chat with Suzanne afterward about her tendency to match-make. She loved the fact that Suzanne was happy Maddie and her brother were dating, but she didn't need her friend to push them together – did she?

Before Maddie could start doubting herself, Luke's voice caught her attention.

"Brad seemed sure of himself today." He shook his head.

"I know." Suzanne's ponytail bounced as she nodded. "I'm glad he didn't win – he was so confident last week as well. He kept boasting about his "lucky" shirt."

Maddie furrowed her brow. Suddenly, references to Brad's "lucky" shirt seemed to be popping up all the time. Was there any significance to it?

Brad had worn his gray shirt with the attractive blue buttons rimmed in gold last Saturday for round one, and again today, for round two – the final round. He hadn't won the competition as he had bragged he would. Maddie assumed it was because his lower score from round one hampered him when the scores for both rounds were taken into account when deciding the winner.

Maddie's thoughts flitted to Ellie. Fred Beldon had seemed pleased that she had won – very pleased. Was there more to their relationship than just barista/customer? Ellie had claimed there wasn't. She seemed gentle and sweet – and Connor appeared to be smitten with her. How could that all be an act?

"Earth to Maddie." Suzanne nudged her.

"Oh – sorry." Maddie looked from Suzanne to Luke and back again. They'd evidently been talking about something but she didn't have a clue what it was.

"Are you okay, Maddie?" Luke looked concerned.

She realized that while she'd been thinking about some of the suspects, the waitress had arrived with their orders and she'd eaten every last scrap of her panini – but if she'd been asked to describe the flavors and textures, she wouldn't have been able to.

Maybe she needed some fresh air.

"I think I'll go and freshen up." She scraped back her chair, the sound lost as the restaurant hummed with the customers' conversation and the chink of cutlery.

"Want some company?" Suzanne offered.

"No, I'll be okay." She smiled at her friend. Maybe all she needed was a few minutes to herself.

She walked to the restroom just down the hall from the coffee shop. What was wrong with her? How could she not focus on Luke sitting next to her? Why was she constantly thinking about the murder? Surely Detective Rawson would be able to solve it.

"Enjoy yourself," she ordered, looking at her reflection in the big mirror in the bathroom. Her amber eyes held a hint of worry, but otherwise she looked normal, apart from a small tangle in her brown shoulder-length hair that she finger-brushed out. She hoped Luke hadn't noticed that.

She allowed herself one last moment to think about what had been nagging her since the final round had ended.

Brad's "lucky" shirt hadn't brought him the luck he'd hoped for – in the first round last weekend, or today's second and final round.

Maddie closed her eyes, trying to remember the first time Brad had mentioned his "lucky" shirt – last Saturday before round one began. And when she and Suzanne had run into him at the burger place on Thursday. And again today, before the beginning of round two.

She gasped as she realized the significance of that shirt. She had to find Detective Rawson and Detective Edgewater right away and tell them what she suspected!

Maddie hurried out of the bathroom and down the hallway toward the small conference room that had hosted the final round an hour earlier. If the detectives were still there, she could give them her information and get back to the coffee shop before Suzanne and Luke missed her.

Pushing the door open, Maddie rushed into the room. The espresso machines were still there, at the individual stations, and so were the black plastic chairs for the audience members, and the long judge's table – but the room was empty. And there hadn't been any sign of the police patrolling the hall, as they had earlier.

Darn! Where could Detective Rawson be? Maybe she should just call the police station and leave a message for him. She reached into her purse for her phone, taking a few steps further into the room. Scanning the room one last time just in case the detective was lurking in a corner – which she knew was a ridiculous thought – she pulled out her cell phone.

"I don't think you'll be needing this." Brad grabbed her cell and threw it across the room before she'd had time to turn it on.

Maddie turned to face him, her eyes wide.

"What do you think you're doing?" she forced her voice to sound calm.

"Stopping you from calling the cops – that's what you were going to do, right?" He scowled at her.

"My friends are in the hotel coffee shop," she informed him, taking a step back. "If I don't return, they'll start looking for me."

"And they'll find you right here." He looked around the room. "It's a shame that idiot Fred Beldon didn't bring his vat of mocha again – maybe he'd finally get the message that his MochLava is only good for drowning people in."

Maddie stifled an indrawn breath. She'd been right! But perhaps there was a chance – a slim one – that Brad didn't know for certain that she knew he was the killer.

That hope was dashed.

"I knew you suspected me after the final round, when that schmuck was teasing me about my lucky shirt," he growled, taking a step toward her. "You looked at me in a weird way, and I thought, *she knows*. So I followed you to the café, and since there's only one way out of there, I waited around the corner." He laughed.

Maddie's spine chilled.

"There's a small lounge area there with a handy wall mirror. I sat in a chair with my back to you, but I could see where you were going thanks to that mirror. And when you headed back here, I knew you were looking for Detective Rawson.

Well, tough luck, sweetie, because he and the other detective have gone back to the precinct. I overheard them when I was checking the scores posted out there." He motioned to the door that Maddie noticed he'd closed.

"Is that why you did it?" Maddie's heart hammered. "Because you don't like Fred Beldon's mocha drink, and you were making a point?"

"No." He chuckled grimly. "I killed Margot Wheeler because she deliberately marked me low in the first round. See, we used to be a couple, but she dumped me last year, after she promised to fund my new coffee importing and roasting business. She knew getting that off the ground would change my life, but she didn't care. Just because she overheard me talking to a buddy about it, telling him I was onto a good thing." He shrugged.

"What about financing it yourself?" Maddie asked in a squeaky voice. If only she could keep him talking, maybe Suzanne and Luke would become worried and look for her.

"I've got bad credit from a mistake I made a few years ago," he gritted. "I tried to get financing after she dumped me, but nobody would lend me the money. So I thought entering this competition would be the solution. I didn't know she would be one of the judges. Once I won and got a spot in the nationals I could parlay that into finally getting financing for my coffee roasting biz. And since I'd probably win the nationals too, I'd be fending off tons of offers. But she wouldn't let that happen." His face changed into a frightening mask.

"I confronted her after round one, demanding to know why she'd marked me so low. She laughed at me." He paused, as if unable to believe that had happened. "She said there was no way I was going to win the competition. That after I'd treated her like a meal ticket, I deserved to lose."

Maddie scanned the room, trying to think of a way out of there. But the only exit was the door – the one that Brad had closed when he'd crept in after her.

"I told her that she owed me, but she kept laughing." His eyes narrowed and his voice hardened. "She shouldn't have done that."

Maddie eyed her phone lying on the floor halfway across the room. If she lunged for it, she'd have to pass Brad. There was no way she would be quick enough.

"What happened then?" Maddie asked, not wanting to know the answer. But if she could distract him for a second, she could make a run for it.

"I pushed her into the vat of mocha. And made sure she stayed in there. Then I ran home and changed my shirt because it had a big splash of that disgusting MochLava on it." He tsked.

Maddie's gaze strayed to his gray shirt, focusing on the second top button. That button was navy. The other buttons on his shirt were mid-blue. That had been what she'd noticed sub-consciously last Saturday, and again today. Each button, even the navy one, was ringed in gold. At first glance, it was hard to tell that specific button was different. But after she saw Brad again last Saturday *after* Margot's death, all the buttons on his shirt had been mid-blue!

"My grandmother gave me this button." He fingered the navy button on his shirt. "Several years ago, the original one came off and Gram said she'd fix it for me. She found this antique button in her box, and said it nearly matched the others." He smirked. "The next day I wore this shirt and won a barista competition, so it became my lucky shirt. And whenever I've worn it, I've either won a competition or placed in the top three."

"And when you came back for round two last Saturday, you wore a shirt similar to that one," Maddie breathed. "Except all the buttons were mid-blue – none were navy."

"Bingo." He pointed his finger at her, gun-style. "I live near here so it was easy to slip out of a side exit, run like my life depended on it–" he snickered "—and swap shirts at my apartment. This shirt is exactly the same as I bought both of them at the same time – except this one has all the original buttons."

"And there weren't any hotel cameras to track you?" Maddie hazarded a guess.

"Nah." He chuckled. "I've been to this hotel before – it hosts a lot of seminars and conventions. It's got limited security cameras in some of the areas, and I know the side exit I used wasn't covered. All I had to say to that stupid detective was that I was in the bathroom – nerves." He smirked. "As if *I* would have nerves. Coffee is my life. I deserved to win. This wasn't exactly my first competition, you know."

"And you're wearing the same "lucky" shirt again today?" Maddie stared at the shirt. Unfortunately she couldn't see a tell-tale mocha splash on it.

"Yep. I washed it three times, got that stain out, and decided to wear it today. With Margot out of the way, I didn't think anyone would stand in my way, and I'd still be able to win the competition." He scowled. "I didn't count on you, Ellie, Connor, and that idiot woman who thinks she's going to get a chain of coffee shops off the ground beating me, even taking into account my lower score from last week.

"It's a shame that Fred Beldon didn't bring that vat today." He glanced casually around the room. "I'll just have to find another way to kill you."

Maddie froze.

How to Move an Object.

The words imprinted themselves in her mind. An image of Trixie, her turquoise eyes glowing, flashed before her eyes.

"Maybe I'll just strangle you." Brad advanced, his large hands flexing.

Maddie recited the words of the spell with all her might – luckily she'd made herself memorize it.

"With a wave of my hand I bid thee *here*!" she muttered fiercely.

She gestured to one of the black plastic chairs in the front row, focusing her mind on the chair hitting Brad and knocking him down.

The black chair rose in the air, hovered, and then struck Brad with a glancing blow.

"Arggh!" He fell to the ground.

Maddie stared as the chair dropped on top of Brad, pinning him in place.

Move!

She sprinted to the door, wrenched it open, and raced down the hall, cannoning into Suzanne and Luke.

"Brad – he's the killer!" She pointed to the room she'd just left, gasping for breath.

"I'll call the police." Luke whipped out his phone.

"We need to get security here until the police arrive," Suzanne said. "Come on!"

Maddie and Suzanne ran down the hall to reception. Maddie cast backward glances toward the hallway, hoping Luke was okay. To her relief, he loped toward them as they explained to the bemused clerk what had just happened, urging her to call security.

"Are you okay, Maddie?" Luke demanded.

Maddie nodded, clutching the edge of the mahogany reception desk for support.

"I pushed some chairs in front of the door so it will take him a while to get out," Luke said. "And I'll go back down there to stand guard until security arrives." He shook his head. "He was babbling about a chair flying through the air and hitting him, and that the chair standing on top of him won't let him get up. He must be concussed."

Suzanne looked sideways at Maddie.

Maddie tried to process what Luke had just told her. She didn't think the spell had included the object pinning a person in place – had she cast it incorrectly, or had Trixie lent her some extra magic?

"Thank goodness you were able to get out of there," Luke continued.

Two security guards came to the desk, asking about the incident. Luke offered to go with them, telling Maddie and Suzanne he'd be back in a few minutes.

"Let's sit down." Suzanne guided Maddie to a vacant sofa near reception.

Maddie sank down into the plush leather, her knees wobbling. Now it was over, everything had seemed to happen quickly and slowly at the same time.

"You cast the How to Move an Object spell," Suzanne whispered in her ear.

Maddie nodded. "Trixie helped – I'm sure of it."

"That's awesome." Suzanne grinned. "But it's not awesome you confronted a killer on your own." She sobered.

Maddie filled in her friend on what had happened, finishing with, "There is no way I would deliberately put myself in danger. I have too much to lose – you,

Trixie, my parents, and—" she paused, "—Luke."

"Good." Suzanne hugged her. "Because I couldn't stand to lose you."

They looked at each other in perfect understanding.

"Okay, ladies." Detective Rawson appeared in front of them, accompanied by Detective Edgewater, his brow furrowed. "Would you mind telling me what's going on?"

CHAPTER 12

"And then I did the How to Move an Object spell," Maddie told Trixie.

The two of them sat on the sofa together, Trixie nestled in Maddie's lap. Suzanne sat next to them, on Maddie's right.

"Mrrow." Trixie sounded pleased.

"Thank you." Maddie pressed her face in the Persian's fur.

"Mrrow." Trixie lifted her head and looked directly at Maddie in complete understanding. No further words were necessary.

After telling Detective Rawson and Detective Edgewater what had happened, watching Brad being marched out of the hotel in handcuffs, and making a formal statement, Luke had driven them back to his house, so Maddie could pick up her car. After kissing her on the forehead and telling her he'd call her tomorrow, he'd waved goodbye to them as they left for Maddie's mom's house.

They picked up Trixie, filled in Mrs. Goodwell quickly about the murder, then Maddie drove the three of them back to her house so they could flop on the sofa and fill in Trixie on everything that had happened – if she didn't know already.

"And the police caught the killer and slapped handcuffs on him," Suzanne added, stroking Trixie.

"Hopefully there won't be any more murders," Maddie said, her tone sincere.

Trixie just looked up at her and blinked. Maddie didn't want to know what *that* meant.

"It's great that you came second," Suzanne said. "Did you see the certificate she won, Trix?"

"Mrrow." Trixie patted Maddie's knee with her paw.

"Yes, I've shown it to her." Maddie smiled.

"Do you want to enter any more barista competitions?" Suzanne asked. "You know I'll be there for you if you do."

"I know. But after today …" Maddie shook her head. "I'm perfectly happy just making coffee for our customers."

"I still think we should frame your certificate and hang it in the truck where all our customers can see it," Suzanne declared.

"Mrrow!"

"It looks like it's two against one." Maddie laughed. "Okay." She didn't think a piece of paper stating she'd come second would entice any new customers to try her coffee – but who knew?

"It's definitely one thing Claudine doesn't have in her coffee shop!" Suzanne's ponytail bounced as she giggled. "Now all we have to do is wait until the full moon next month and find out which new spell will be revealed to you."

***

The following Tuesday, just after the early morning rush had abated, two new customers stood at the serving window. Ellie and Connor.

"Hi," Ellie said shyly.

"Cool truck." Connor grinned.

"Hey, you two." Suzanne stuck her head out of the window. "It's great to see you. What are you doing here?"

"Mrrow?" Trixie looked up from washing her paw, tilting her head as she looked at the newcomers.

"Hi." Maddie hopped off her stool and came to the window.

"Ohhh, your cat is gorgeous," Ellie murmured.

"Mrrow." Trixie sat up straight and gazed at Ellie in fascination.

"This is Trixie." Maddie introduced them.

Connor smiled at the Persian.

"Congratulations again for Saturday," Maddie told Ellie.

"Thanks." Ellie touched her earring, which Maddie noted was a bluebird with accents of silver.

"We've got some exciting news." Connor wrapped his arm around Ellie. "Diana Swift offered us both jobs!"

"You didn't get a job offer from Fred Beldon?" Suzanne asked curiously.

"No, why would I?" Ellie crinkled her brow. "I couldn't work in a factory making that awful mocha beverage." She shuddered.

"Yep, it was pretty terrible." Suzanne laughed.

"Our new jobs are thanks to you, Suzanne," Connor continued. "Because of what you said on Saturday about how cool it would be if Diana offered both of us jobs. So after the competition, Diana told Ellie she needed an answer in the next few days, and Ellie—" he looked at her proudly "—asked if the position could be split in two. And Diana agreed."

"I'll be creating the speciality drinks and be in charge of the roasting and sourcing," Ellie spoke up. "And Connor will head up training and development."

"Although the salary each will be less than she quoted Ellie in the beginning because now there are two of us doing what was supposed to be one job, the pay and benefits are a bit better than what we're getting now."

"And I'll get to do everything I love about being a barista." Ellie's eyes sparkled.

"I enjoy training the new baristas where I'm currently working," Connor said. "So it's a win for both of us."

Maddie and Suzanne congratulated them again, Trixie adding a happy "Mrrow."

"I'd love to try your mocha, Maddie," Ellie said in a soft voice.

"Me too," Connor added. "I was only one point behind you after the final round."

"Sure." Maddie smiled at them, hoping they wouldn't be disappointed. She was thrilled Diana's job offer had worked out for both of them. Maybe it was time for her and Suzanne to start working on a business plan if they were serious about expanding one day.

The espresso machine hissed and burred as Maddie set to work. After she poured the regular mochas, she placed them on the serving hatch.

"On the house," she said as Connor dug into his jeans pocket for his wallet.

"Are you sure?" Ellie asked.

"Definitely." Suzanne's ponytail bounced.

Maddie, Suzanne, and Trixie watched as Ellie and Connor took their first sips.

A smile stole across Ellie's face and she turned to Connor.

A matching smile creased his expression.

"You have a gift, Maddie," Ellie said softly.

"Thank you," Maddie replied.

"Yeah." Connor took another sip. "This totally rocks."

"Thanks," Maddie said again, pleased that these two skilled baristas enjoyed her coffee.

"Maybe one day you'll have a whole fleet of coffee trucks." Ellie smiled.

"Maybe," Maddie echoed, wondering if she would ever be ready for *that.*

"Perhaps we can send our baristas to you for training, Connor." Suzanne giggled.

"Just let me know." Connor grinned.

The four of them laughed, Trixie adding a happy "Mrrow,".

Maddie couldn't help thinking that right now, life was just about perfect.

The End

I hope you enjoyed reading this mystery. Sign up to my newsletter at **www.JintyJames.com** and be among the first to discover when the next book will be published!

Have you read:

Spells and Spiced Latte – A Coffee Witch Cozy Mystery – Maddie Goodwell 1

Visions and Vanilla Cappuccino – A Coffee Witch Cozy Mystery – Maddie Goodwell 2

Enchantments and Espresso - A Coffee Witch Cozy Mystery – Maddie Goodwell 4

Cacao Orange Health Ball recipe on the next page in US and Metric measurements!

CACAO ORANGE HEALTH BALLS (US MEASUREMENTS)

12 fresh Medjool dates, pitted
6 Tablespoons almond meal
Zest of one large orange
2 Tablespoons cacao powder
4 Tablespoons maple syrup
Shredded or desiccated coconut (optional)

Place all ingredients except coconut in a food processor. Whiz until well combined and the mixture comes together – it should be like a thick paste.

Roll into small balls, then roll into the coconut if desired.

Refrigerate for one – two hours to set.

Best eaten day made.

Note 1: If you don't have cacao powder, you can use cocoa instead. The flavor might be a little different, but the balls should still be delicious!

Note 2: No matter how much you process the mixture, you might still have some harder bits of date in it that seem a little "stalky" in your mouth. That was Suzanne's experience, anyway!

CACAO ORANGE HEALTH BALLS (METRIC MEASUREMENTS)

12 fresh Medjool dates, pitted
66g almond meal
Zest of one large orange
30mls cacao powder
60mls maple syrup
Shredded or desiccated coconut
(optional)

Place all ingredients except coconut in a food processor. Whiz until well combined and the mixture comes together – it should be like a thick paste.

Roll into small balls, then roll into the coconut if desired.

Refrigerate for one – two hours to set.

Best eaten day made.

Note 1: If you don't have cacao powder, you can use cocoa instead. The flavor might be a little different, but the balls should still be delicious!

Note 2: No matter how much you process the mixture, you might still have some harder bits of date in it that seem a little "stalky" in your mouth. That was Suzanne's experience, anyway!

Made in United States
North Haven, CT
02 December 2023

44894047R00150